Young Love

Paige Powers

Young Love

Copyright 2014 Paige Powers,

Dipasha Tara Raj Publications House

Table of Contents

Chapter 1

Lidia

I walked to his house smiling. It was a sunny day. The birds were singing, the sky was clear and it was warm even though it was September. I spun the ring Grant had given me, around on my finger. We had been together for one whole year, and it wasn't an on and off thing. He was the love of my life. My life was perfect right now. My best friend Kendra and I were closer than ever. I didn't really like her boyfriend, though. In fact, we hated each other. But that didn't stop the four of us from doing everything together! Double dates every weekend! Drives to the beach in the summer. Everything! My parents were great! They let me do anything I wanted. They loved Grant, too.

And today was, well, my seventeenth birthday and I wondered what Grant had planned. Maybe a party? A romantic picnic under the stars? Maybe we would take our relationship to the next level. Maybe I was ready. I sighed and grinned up at the evening sun. My heart thudded excitedly in my chest as I thought of the possibilities. My thoughts wandered to Kendra and the time I talked to her about Grant and me. She and her annoying boyfriend Jack were a cute couple, but she had mentioned breaking up with him when Grant and I were having a rough patch a couple of months ago, although she never did. She just seemed distant these past few days. It was strange. I'd known her all my life but she wouldn't open up to me; she'd just tell me it was nothing. The funny thing was, when we were freshmen in high school, we fought over Grant. He was the famous football player that every girl had a crush on. We told each other dreams we had of him and which hair dye we thought would make him look like Zac Efron. Those were the good old days. But when Grant asked me to homecoming in my junior year, Kendra never said anything about him after that.

A couple months later she met Jack, a new student. One look at him and I knew he was going to be trouble. And trouble, he was!

He was sent to the principal's office on the first day of school for talking back to a teacher. I told her he wasn't a good idea but she seemed to really like him so I never said anything again.

I was one house away from Grant's when someone hit my shoulder. "Owe!" I complained and jumped away from the person. "Jack!" I said narrowing my eyes, annoyed. His dark blue eyes looked black under his brown bangs and his brown hair looked messy the way guys wore their hair nowadays. He also had on his favorite black leather jacket which was something he wore every day. It was so annoying!

"Well it's good to see you, too, Princess!" He smirked. I glared deeply at him because I hated it when he called me that. I wasn't a cheerleader and neither was I a popular girl. I didn't even want to be one. But he didn't care.

"What are you doing here?" I growled. He grinned.

"Going to see my girlfriend. She wanted to talk to me. Is that OK, Lidia?" he said, pointing to Kendra's house which was next to Grant's. They had been neighbors for two years.

"You better not hurt my best friend, Jack, or else you're dead meat," I said, staring him down which made him grin even more. If that's possible. I had said this exact same thing to him probably a million times now. Not that he had any regard for it.

"No problem, Princess!" he slapped my shoulder in a playful way.

"Ass," I muttered and moved past him and on to Grant's porch. I put on a smile for Grant and knocked on his door. It swung open and there was Grant, looking like Adonis, wearing faded jeans and a white T- shirt. His blonde hair was slicked to the side and his brown eyes smiled with his lips. Before he could say anything, I reached up and pulled his lips to mine. He tasted of Spearmint. He pulled me in as we kissed and shut the door with his foot. Our tongues twirled together and he pulled back.

"What's wrong?" I asked frowning. His eyes looked sad but I didn't understand.

"Nothing, it's just….don't want to get too carried away." I smiled.

"You're right," I leaned up and touched my lips to his ear. "We always have later." I heard him swallow and I smiled as I looked back at him.

"I made supper," he said. His voice was hoarse. I grinned.

"Come on!"

We ate in silence, across from each other. His parents were out for the weekend, as always, so we had the house to ourselves except for the maid who was cleaning upstairs. His parents were rich, so he always got what he wanted. He looked a little nervous and I just grinned to myself, hoping he was nervous for the same reason I was. Finally Grant put his fork down and looked at me.

"Um, Lidia, can we go into the living room to talk?" I curiously wiped my mouth and stood up. We walked into the big living room and he sat down on the sofa first. I sat down beside him and looked at him, feeling a little worried.

"What's wrong?" I asked. He looked away from my eyes and took my hand.

"Ollie," he said, looking up at me and calling me by my nickname. My heart gave a quick thud. I loved it when he called me that! It was so cute! "You know that we have been dating for a year now, right?" I nodded and smiled.

"And I loved every minute of it!" I exclaimed. Why did this conversation seem as if something bad was about to happen?

"Yes, I did too," he said nodding. "But…."

"But, what?" I asked quickly. He looked at me with sad eyes.

"Ollie, I think it's time we break up."

Jack

Kendra had called and asked if I could come over. Her sister was at work. I grinned to myself because we always made out on the sofa or on her bed when her sister was not home. Of course I wanted more, but Kendra didn't want to, so I never pushed. She was a great girlfriend, but sometimes I thought we didn't click so much; and she was always talking about herself. I guess that's what I get for dating a cheerleader. I walked down the street to her house which wasn't far from my own. I would have driven but the last time I did, Kendra's sister came in and practically screamed her head off when she found me hiding in Kendra's closet. So this time, if she came home early, I could hide without her finding out that I was even there. Kendra's sister didn't like me very much and I wondered why. I was an awesome guy!

On the way to Kendra's house, while deep in thought, I bumped into someone, only to find out that it was Lidia. She jumped and looked at me, her green eyes sparkling in the sun. "Jack!" she said, looking quite annoyed. See, what I didn't like about Lidia was that she didn't like me. I mean every girl loved me! But I couldn't woo her; which was probably why I was so attracted to her. She had a great ass too! "Well it's good to see you, too, Princess!" I said with a smirk. I gave her that name because she hated it and I loved to tease her! It became a hobby. She looked kind of sexy as she glared at me, her blonde hair falling in ringlets around her face. Kendra was my girlfriend, but I could look and flirt as much as I wanted. I just couldn't touch.

"What're you doing here?" she growled. She looked pretty hot in a pair of dark jeans and a light blue top. I pointed to Kendra's house next to Grant's.

"Going to see my girlfriend. She wanted to talk to me. Is that okay, Lidia?"

"You better not hurt my best friend, Jack, or else you're dead meat," she threatened. I smirked again just to tease her. She and Kendra were pretty close.

"No problem, Princess!" I slapped her shoulder like I would to my guy friends. She was pretty tall for a girl so I didn't have to reach down or anything. She rolled her eyes.

"Ass," she muttered. I smirked as she turned away to leave and I watched her butt swing as she walked off. I bit my lip. Nah, Kendra's better, I thought as I walked up the steps of Kendra's house. I knocked twice before she opened the door. She was wearing a short skirt and a low cut T-shirt and she wore her black hair long and straight.

"Ah, already dressed for the occasion," I said, looking her over. I walked in and shut the door. I grabbed her waist as she smirked, then pulled her against me and kissed her. She seemed distracted as I put my hand under her shirt wanting to get it off a little.

"Jack," she said and pulled back. I looked at her. "Um, actually, I wanted to talk to you about something," she said. I was puzzled.

"OK? But can it wait till after I'm done?" I said kissing her neck. She took a deep breath and shook her head, pushing me away from her.

"Come on," she said, dragging me inside the house.

"Oh, yeah, the sofa's much better!" I said as she guided me to the chair.

"No, no. We need to talk," she said seriously. I looked into her eyes and suddenly I was worried.

"What's this about, Kendra?" I demanded. She sat down on a white chair and looked at me.

"Jack, I really like you..but...," she looked down and pushed back her hair. Great. I knew where she was going with this. "I'm breaking up with you."

Damn I hated those words!

Chapter 2

Lidia

I couldn't remember what happened next. I recalled throwing the ring he had given me, slapping him and screaming at him that he just had to break up with me on my birthday. The bastard just shrugged! I stormed out of the house, rage engraved on my face. I had to talk to my best friend! Tears were already forming in my eyes as I stomped my feet over the front porch of her house. Before I could do anything, the door flew open and Jack, his face red and his blue eyes blazing, stomped past me and I frowned in bewilderment.

"Jack!" Kendra yelled but stopped when she saw me. She looked like chaos.

"Oh Kendra!" I whispered. She looked at my eyes and her face became saddened. "He broke up with me," I choked. She embraced me but didn't look surprised. I cried on her shoulder. "I-I-I don't know what I did wrong."

She rubbed my back not saying a word. "I mean, I was thinking we had really been in love. What changed his mind?" I wiped my nose and Kendra retreated. Her face was guilty.

"Olli, listen..," she looked away, her eyes glistening with tears.

"What?" I asked. She looked up at me.

"Grant broke up with you because….because we wanted to be together." I was speechless. My mouth wouldn't move, my legs became jelly. "Ollie?" she asked looking concerned. I looked past her. How long had they liked each other? How long had he been cheating on me? I knew she didn't say it…but I realized then, that he was always going home early… getting off work late…not coming over on Friday nights when Kendra's sister was out….it all made sense. "Lidia?" Kendra whispered. "I'm so, so, so sorry. It just happened! I didn't mean to hurt you. It...it's complicated." My hands curled into fists at my sides. "Ollie?" she asked. I turned on the step and walked down the stairs. "Lidia!" she called. I ignored· her and started running down the walkway, tears streaming down my cheeks. I finally ran to my favorite place which was overgrown with vines and trash. My swing set was still there with vines creeping on it and the rust falling off with just one touch. Two swings were all that were left of the swing set. Beside it there was a slide and a wooden seesaw. I opened the gate, walked in, sat in my swing and rocked back and forth; the breeze blowing my hair back.

"Oh...sorry," I looked up to the corner of the park and saw Jack coming in. I stared at him for a while and he looked up. Something turned in my stomach but I ignored it. Instead I snorted.

"Doesn't matter. I've already lost all my dignity." I said wiping my eyes with the back of my hand. He smiled but his eyes weren't happy. "You can come in I don't care," I said and started to swing lightly. He climbed up the steps and sat at the top of the slide. "You know it's not safe up there," I said not really caring. He looked down at me with a smug look.

"Doesn't matter now, does it?" he asked, clearly tired. I looked away from his eyes and down on the ground.

"Grant broke up with me," I whispered not sure if he heard me. Jack sighed.

"Kendra broke up with me."

I glanced up at him. He was looking at the darkening sky with a sad look. Wow, that was the first time I actually saw him without a grin or smug look. It actually made me sad to see him like that. Ugh! Get some backbone girl! He doesn't care how you're feeling.

"I might hate you but I don't have anyone else to talk to," I said quietly. I could see him nod. "What makes me feel even more pathetic is that he and Kendra were seeing each other for, hell, I don't know how long!" I said with a cold laugh. Jack looked down at me, his eyes wide and his teeth clenched.

"Bitch!" he yelled. I flinched slightly.

"She didn't tell you?" I asked stopping my swing. He looked back down at me.

"No! She told me she was breaking up with me. But she didn't tell me she was with Grant! Bitch!" he yelled again. I smirked.

"She didn't say but...now I remember all the times Grant cancelled...because he was seeing her." Jack looked at me. He actually seemed kind.

"Yeah, I see it too. She would kick me out early on Fridays saying her sister was coming home...but then she would call later that night saying her sister didn't come home till midnight...I can't believe she would do that!" He looked disgusted. "I mean, no offense, but I look so much better then Grant!" I had just started to nod my head, but then I stopped and glared at him.

"Hey! You jerk! You're not that good looking!" I said, standing up. He smirked down at me.

"Besides you, Taylor, everyone likes me." He gave me a wink and jumped off the slide. He liked calling me by my last name, Taylor. I shook my head.

"That's because I have more brains then the bimbos that like you." He stopped and glanced at me with his eyes narrowed. It was my turn to smirk. He looked away and sighed.

"I never cheated on Kendra. I could never do that to her," he said quietly. I wasn't sure I'd heard him correctly.

"I guess that's what I get," I whispered near tears again.

"What?" Jack asked.

"I failed my last history course and bribed Mr. Barns to give me a D." Jack looked at me his eyebrow going up. Finally, he burst out laughing. I frowned.

"What?" I demanded and walked over to him. He (of laughter, of course) as he looked at me while holding

"Wow, Lidia!" he said straightening up. "What Dude, my parents would have killed me if they kn..... . ... defensively. His lips quivered.

"I'm sorry, but seriously, if you think this is what you get for bribing Mr. Barns, I don't know what's in store for me!"

"Probably jail," I grinned. He stopped laughing and glared at me.

"Cry, baby," I joked.

"Pansy," he said, raising an eyebrow.

"Touché," I smirked but sighed. I crossed my arms over my chest.

"I better go," I said. He nodded and suddenly it was quiet. I looked up at him and bit at my lip. He was looking at me. His eyes were different. Softer? Kinder? His eyes seemed to gleam in the dusk to dawn light above the small park. "I'll see you tomorrow," I said quickly. He nodded and looked away looking a little red. Red?

"Bye."

I went past him and out of the park. I closed the small gate and realized that my heart had been pounding in my chest. I took a deep breath. Jack was okay today but I still hated his guts. I walked home alone in the dark.

Jack

I walked home late that night, feeling depressed. I hated Kendra right now. She was such a cold-hearted bitch! I didn't know what I actually saw in her! Oh wait, yeah I do. Great boobs and great ass! But I have to say that Lidia has a better one. Even if she doesn't try to show it with the baggy jeans.

I walked into my house after opening all the locks. I closed them all and went to my room. My mom was home watching TV in the living room with a box of ice cream. "Oh, hey, honey!" she said, her voice hyper.

"Hi," I mumbled and went into my small room. It had a double bed, a dresser and a desk full of junk. I never used it. I hated school. I couldn't wait to get out! Which would thankfully be next year.

"Honey, is something wrong?" my mom asked, standing by my door. She was a petite woman with dark blonde hair and blue eyes like mine. She was always going on dates. She really was a great mom.

"Yeah, um, Kendra broke up with me." I scratched the back of my neck, avoiding her gaze.

"Aw, honey," she said and put the box of ice cream on my desk to come over and give me a hug. I wrapped my arms around her small frame and sighed. I knew if Lidia saw this she would die laughing. I loved my mom more than anything in the world. Since my dad left when I was 10, I've had to take care of her. She pulled back. "Don't worry, baby. There are more fishes in the sea. And with your mommy's good looks, you've already got a hundred lined up!" That made me laugh.

"Thanks, mom. It's just that..she..she cheated on me," I said. She gasped.

"Kendra? The good girl? Oh my gosh! She never seemed the type to me." I shrugged.

"I just wish I could get back at her. She really hurt me." Mom sighed and slapped my shoulder.

"You don't need to baby. Just find another girl you like and go out with her. She'll get jealous and run back to you. Don't worry!" She walked out humming a song. I frowned at the pile of clothes in the corner. Find another girl and make her jealous. Um, sounds like a good idea to me. But I don't like any of those dumb girls at school. I need to find a girl that is going to kill Kendra when she sees me with her. Someone who will go with it and won't get attached to me. That will just be in it to get back at her…then it hit me and I grinned so wide my jaws hurt.

"Lidia!" I said out loud. Perfect! She and I could pretend to be together and do stuff to make Kendra come back to me! It's a perfect plan! But will Lidia agree to it? I licked my lips in wonder. She would be fun to kiss and just to see the look on Kendra's face…priceless!

I'd do anything to get Lidia to do it. "Hey, Mom?" I called.

"Yeah?" she asked.

"What's with the ice cream?" I heard her giggle. "New guy?" I asked.

"Yep!" she sounded like a little girl again.

Chapter 3

Lidia

I woke up that morning to find black makeup smeared under my eyes and my eyes red and puffy. Ugh, I hated break ups! Even though this was my second one. The first time it wasn't bad 'because we'd only been dating a month.

I got in the shower and threw on a pair of loose jeans and a red and black shirt afterwards. I slipped on a pair of sandals and walked out the door with a piece of toast in my mouth and hopped into my black jeep. I hadn't seen my parents in about two days. They'd gone to Ireland for a little getaway, as they usually did. I didn't mind, it's just that things usually got a little lonely at the house. But when Grant and I were together it was perfectly okay with me because we wanted to be left alone. I sniffed. Don't cry! Do not cry! I commanded myself. I turned on the radio and pulled into the school's parking lot. I took a deep breath and got out.

I went to my locker, trying not to look at anyone. I knew if everyone found out, they would all be trying to get the details of what really happened. I didn't want to talk about it. I put my books in my locker and shut it.

"Taylor!" I turned around and knew who it was because only Jack called me by my last name.

"What?" I asked with a sigh. He actually looked good today. The ends of his hair were wet from a shower and his blue eyes looked lighter today. Why are you thinking that way? That's disgusting. You know that, right? I shook myself mentally.

"I need to talk to you," he said quietly, putting on a seductive look. I didn't fall for it.

"Don't play with me Jack. What do you want?" He smirked.

"Grumpy, aren't we?" I rolled my eyes.

"Why aren't you? Your girlfriend just broke up with you!" He just shrugged.

"Oh, well. Listen, I was thinking last night—."

"Finally figured out how to do that?" I teased and he scowled.

"And I really want Kendra back. And I know you want Grant back. Am I right?" I looked away. Yes, of course I wanted him back! I loved him. "So, my mom gave me an idea." I looked up at him, finally getting a little intrigued. "Let's make them jealous!" I stared at him a moment as he grinned like an idiot.

"And how would we do that?" He sighed and rolled his eyes.

"We become a couple and fake a relationship. It's perfect! They'll see us together and then they'll want us back! I'm genius!" He jumped up and down and spun around trying not to hit anyone and looked at me. I stared wide eyed at him. Surprised.

"So?"

"So what?" I was still reeling from the suggestion. He frowned slightly.

"Are you in?"

I pondered it. It was a great plan actually. But I didn't want to lie! And would Grant really want me back? If he saw me with Jack, would he care? Would he be jealous?

"I don't know." He put his arms down.

"Lidia! Come on!"

I remembered when Grant and I were on the beach in California. He'd lay beside me and look at me with love in his eyes.

"I love you, Ollie," he'd said. I'd looked at him and smiled.

"I love you, too," I kissed him and put my hand on his bare chest.

"I'll always love you," he'd said before kissing my nose. I smiled.

"Lidia?" I blinked and looked at Jack in front of me. My classmates passed me but didn't seem to care. I looked out the doors of the school and saw a couple holding hands, walking through the doors. My heart slowly stopped.

"Grant," I said and Jack looked in the same direction. His eyes widened. Kendra and Grant held hands smiling like they just won the lottery. Everyone stopped and looked at them, then Jack and I. I looked down. Everyone will know the whole story by the end of the day. Grant and Kendra walked past us and Kendra smiled at me. Grant finally looked at me and smiled. I glared.

"Hey," Kendra said to us.

"Bitch," Jack muttered. She gasped quietly. Everyone had stopped talking and was watching us. She glared at Jack and I fought the urge to laugh. They went past and disappeared into the crowd. "So, anyhow," Jack said looking at me as I watched them. "Are you in or out?"

I couldn't believe he had the guts to do this to me! After everything we had been through! What a bastard. I looked at Jack and smiled evilly.

"I'm in."

He grinned.

"I'll come over later and we'll talk more." He said and quickly hurried off to class. I stood there still thinking about breaking Grant's heart. Wait, what heart? It wasn't like it he still had feelings for me. Or did he? Man, did I hope he did.

I went ahead of Jack and he followed me to my house in his orange '73 Camaro. It looked like a piece of junk. People at school made fun of him about it, but he didn't seem to care. But whenever some kid called him trailer trash, he gave him a black eye. I never questioned why, but Kendra said it was because he was really sensitive about that kind of stuff. He was the bad boy. The rich boy who never got attention from his parents. At least that's what everyone said. I didn't know and I really didn't care. I pulled into the house and got out. Jack got out as well and looked up at my suburb home. He smiled. He had visited once or twice and always made fun of me. It was totally not like me. I unlocked the door and walked in. It was quiet except for the humming of the big fish tank in the living room.

"Where are your parents?" Jack asked as he entered, scaring me a little. I put my hand to my forehead.

"Um, Ireland I think." He raised an eyebrow at me before dropping his backpack on the sofa. "Yeah. Are you thirsty?" I asked, going up the stairs. He followed.

"Nope," he said looking around. I walked to my room and put my bag on my bed. "Nice room," he said from the door. He leaned on the frame and looked around. It was a mess. I never cleaned it. It had old band posters over the red peeling paint. The new ones were the collection of pictures I'd taken on my trip to Greece.

"Cool pictures," he commented. I nodded.

"Yeah, my parents sent me there for my birthday."

"Mm," he said.

"So, what do you think we should talk about?" I asked sitting down on my bed. He still stood at the door. "You can come in, you know?" He looked back at me and smiled a little. My stomach fluttered. I wanted to slap at it but stopped myself from making a fool of myself.

"Thanks," he came in and sat down at my computer chair. He rotated it and turned to face me.

"What?" I asked.

"I think we should probably wait a day or two before we show up at school as 'a couple'." He used his fingers to stress the quotes. I nodded.

"Agreed." It was silent. "So, what do you think we should do? Like should we sit with them? How are we going to make them jealous?" He looked at me and winked. I rolled my eyes.

"We make them jealous by acting like a perfect couple and like nothing happened." He came over to the bed and sat down looking me in the eyes. I sighed.

"I can't believe I'm doing this," I said closing my eyes for a second. He snorted.

"Like it's going to be a stroll in the park for me!" I gasped.

"So, what are you saying? I'm not a fun person?" He shrugged and looked away, about to laugh. "Ass!" I yelled. This time he laughed.

"I just want to make them jealous so we can get back to the way things were," I said.

"Simple." He nodded and looked at me, his eyes alight.

"We should make out in front of them!" I laughed.

"Yeah right! Like I'm really going to kiss you!" He looked hurt for a moment but quickly recovered.

"How else are we going to make them jealous? Or pose as a real couple?" he questioned, throwing his hands in the air. I frowned.

"I don't know, but I want to wait the longest I can!" He rolled his eyes, annoyed.

"Fine, then," he slapped his hand down on my thigh and I jumped. He looked over at me. "We'll have to use body language." I looked down at his hand and up at his eyes. He smirked. I didn't move his hand…it felt kind of good….he looked surprised that I didn't, and decided to get as far as he could. His hand went up a little further and my heart rate started to build. I wanted to slap his hand. I wanted to slap his face but I couldn't. I could hear his breath becoming heavy as we both watched his hand. His hand was warm on my cold leg. I clenched my teeth. Come on Lidia! He's taking advantage of you! His hand made its way lower on my thigh and my body was heating up. Finally, I grabbed his hand and for a second or two we looked at each other. I stood up dropping his hand, not knowing what came over me.

"You are such a jerk," I said, pushing back my hair, trying to cool down. He smirked.

"Maybe you should even change your wardrobe a little. You know, spice things up a bit." He stood up in front of me and looked me over once. "If you're dating me, you have to look good."

I scowled.

"Yeah, someone has to look good in the relationship."

He snorted.

"Whatever, Taylor," he walked past me into the hall. I ran out after catching my breath.

"Wait! What do I do?" I asked. He stopped on the stairs and turned to me.

"I'll come and pick you up on Wednesday and we'll officially be a couple. We'll go to school and wing it. If anyone asks, say you've always had a crush on me and that after Grant broke up with you, you finally decided to give in to your love for me." He fluttered his eye lashes. I crossed my arms and rolled my eyes.

"I'm definitely not saying that! I'll figure out something else."

He shrugged.

"Whatever, you want, Princess," he called as he turned and continued walking down the stairs. "See ya!"

He slammed the front door and I heard his car start up. I took a deep breath and sat down on the steps. 'Oh my gosh Lidia! Why would you let him feel you up like that? Touch you like that! Why would you?' I yelled at myself. I could still feel his warm hand on me and I shook my head trying to get the feeling away. 'He's a jerk! You don't like him. You are repelled by him! I can do this. Just a week or two and Grant will be my boyfriend again. You can handle this. You can handle this.' I repeated to myself. I stood up and went back to my room to study for my English paper.

Chapter 4

Next Day

School went pretty bad. Everyone was asking questions about Grant and me.

"Oh why did he break up with you?" "Aw sweetie I'm so sorry!" "He's such a jerk! I don't know why you ever went out with him in the first place." And then there was a rumor going around that he broke up with me because I wouldn't 'do it'. It was a load of rubbish! I was sick of it! Jack and I didn't talk or even really look at each other. We both knew we needed to have our freedom until the next day. I got home and sighed as I went into my room. My cell rang and I picked it up.

"What?" I asked annoyed.

"Oh is that how you treat your fake boyfriend now?" I closed my eyes and sighed once again.

"Jack," I said.

"Lidia," I could hear the amusement in his voice. "I'm coming to pick you up about 7am tomorrow so be ready." He said sternly. Like a father.

"And what if I'm not?" I challenged. He seemed shocked to hear me say that.

"Do you want to know if you don't?" he threatened. His voice was so calm and seductive. I decided I didn't.

"Whatever, bye."

"Wear something good tomorrow, OK?" he teased. I almost gasped again. I stared angrily at the wall ahead of me.

"I'll wear what I freaking want to!" I yelled and hung up. I shook my head biting my lip. What's so wrong with my clothes? I looked down at my pants and stood up. I went to my full length mirror and saw the baggy jeans sliding off my hips. My shirt had paint splotches on it. Maybe I do need to get some more clothes. I thought of Grant and Kendra together. My eyes narrowed as I grabbed my keys and my parents' credit card and left for the mall.

A lady from my favorite shop helped me pick out some good clothes for my body type. She said I was the perfect shape for a pretty short red and white polka-dot summer dress. I think I fell in love with it before I even put it on. They only had one in stock.

"Oh my gosh! It's perfect! I knew it would fit you! And it's the last one." I twirled in the mirror looking like a model. I hate my baggy jeans. I smiled.

"I'll take it." The lady picked out millions of jeans and basically tore off the jeans I was wearing. She picked out a whole bunch of tight pretty and skimpy shirts. I planned to throw out my old clothes and replace them with my new ones. These were better. I hated wearing clothes like this but now I didn't care. I wanted to impress Grant and make him want me back. He's going to want me back for sure. Once he sees me in that red dress….he'll be totally mine! I looked in the mirror. I was going to be sexy Lidia Taylor tomorrow.

I heard the car door shut and raced across the room to look out the window. Jack walked up to the door wearing his famous black leather jacket with his hair messy in a good way. The doorbell rang and I grinned as I grabbed my new purse and put on my Aviator sunglasses as I headed down the stairs. I almost tripped in the black boots I was wearing. I took a deep breath, then opened the door and struck a sexy pose. Jack was looking at something but quickly averted his eyes to me. His blue eyes were wide and he looked me over a couple of times.

"Lidia?" he asked. I grinned as I put up my sunglasses.

"Yes?" I asked, my voice high pitched, more girly. I'd decided to wear a pair of tight black jeans and a red strapless shirt with a big bow on my left breast. And a pair of high black boots. His eyes were as wide as I ever saw them.

"Damn, Taylor!" he said as I moved past him.

"Eat your heart out," I said and put down my sunglasses. I heard him laugh and run after me. He grabbed my waist before I could get in the car and pushed me up against it, turning me to face him. I gasped. "Get off me!" He looked down on me, his hands still on my waist. He was about two inches taller than me, maybe less, so we were almost at eye level. He looked into my eyes and wiggled his eyebrows.

"You're looking hot today. I've done well."

I rolled my eyes but they were wasted on him since I had sunglasses on. His leg moved between my legs and my breath caught. "Now if we can get you going…." I pushed him back and he laughed. "Kidding!" he said, putting his hands up in surrender.

"Whatever! Let's just go so we can get this over with." I got in his car and we drove off. Jack kept looking at me as we drove and when we got to the school's parking lot, I slung my backpack over my shoulder as we walked towards the school building. Jack sighed.

"You're right. I can't believe we're doing this," he mumbled. I nodded and reached to grab his hand but he jerked it away.

"Give me your damn hand!" I muttered as people started to see us. He rolled his eyes and took my hand. Surprisingly they fit together perfectly. 'Don't get any ideas Lidia,' I scolded myself. While walking, I felt his arm brush against mine. People gaped at us as we walked up the steps.

"Hey man!" Jack called and waved to a friend of his. I smiled and calmly walked beside him. We went inside and everyone stopped to look directly at us. They started to whisper as I took off my sunglasses.

"Who's the hot chick?"

"Is she new?"

"Dude, I bet she's from France!"

"Man I'd like to tap that!" the murmurs were all around. I felt good today. I felt confident. Jack walked me to my locker and spun me around. I wanted to yell but saw eyes on us.

"Honey," Jack said in a sweet voice.

"Yes, baby?" I asked touching his arm. He looked surprised and cleared his throat.

"I'll take your books so you don't have to worry about them,"

I smiled.

"Sure," I smirked as I handed over all my books to him. They were heavy and he grunted slightly.

"Come on," he muttered. I took his hand which unbalanced him but I didn't care; I wasn't carrying my books.

Chapter 5

People asked us all sorts of questions. It was interesting to see their reaction to us as a couple. It was even more interesting to see how surprised they were about the change in me.

"I changed because I wanted the best for my baby." I squeezed Jack's cheek causing him to smile painfully and glare at me as they looked away. Next was lunch. We hadn't seen Grant and Kendra but we were informed that they knew. We were the talk of the school. So before we went into the cafeteria I pushed Jack in a hall without kids and sighed. "Man, this is so tiring."

"You think?" he said as I massaged his hand. I grinned.

"You squeezed it so hard I thought I was going to lose it."

"Oh get over it, baby," I teased.

He looked at me.

"I like it when you call me that." He winked and I rolled my eyes.

"Tell me again why I wanted to do this?"

He thought for a moment. "Because you're truly and madly in love with me deep down?"

"Nah," I snorted.

He frowned and pouted.

"Come on, I look good today. For you."

"You don't look that good," he said. I laughed.

I grabbed his hand and he winced. I loosened my grip. "Come on." We went into the cafeteria and took a deep breath. There, in the corner, were Kendra and Grant. They were feeding each other pudding. Ew! "Let's get something first and then we'll go over there," I said. He nodded and stared at them as we got in line. I hit him in the ribs.

"Owe!" he complained.

"Pay attention to me!" I muttered. He laughed and then I could feel his breath on my neck.

"Why? Are you jealous?" Goose-bumps rose on my arms and I tried to act like it didn't bother me. What are you talking about? It didn't! Of course it didn't...why would it?

"Ew, no!" I said and laughed. We got our food and walked to their table.

"Hey guys!" I said cheerily. They both looked up at us with wide eyes. Especially at me. Kendra had a spoonful of pudding on its way into Grant's mouth but it dropped to the table.

"Lidia?" they both asked. Jack put his hand around my waist as I gave them my best smile. Grant's eyes glazed over as he looked at me.

"Yeah silly! Hey can Jack and I sit with you guys?"

Kendra's eyes went to Jack and they bulged while Grant, suddenly looking parched, drank his water.

"What…." She stammered.

"Oh! Sorry, Kendra. I totally forgot to tell you! Jack and I are together now."

Grant suddenly spat out his water and some came out through his nose. Jack swallowed a laugh but I could feel his body shaking a little.

"You're what?" they both exclaimed, staring at us. I smiled.

"Aw, you didn't know?" They both shook their heads dumbly. "Jack asked me out as soon as Kendra dumped him." Jack bumped me in a rough way. I smirked slightly. "So, we're together now. Can we sit here?" I asked sliding into a seat next to Grant. He still stared at me dumbfounded. Jack took the seat next to Kendra. He didn't even look at her. I could see a vein on his neck bulge as I looked up at him but he didn't even look up.

"Jack, baby?" he finally looked up. His eyes were a little sad but something wasn't right.

"Yeah?" he asked.

"You want to come over after school? Remember, my parents are gone. It'll be fun."

He smirked a little. "Sure."

I frowned slightly then turned and smiled at Grant. It wasn't as hard as I thought it would be to see him. I started to eat and felt uneasy about why Jack wasn't talking. But who cares! I'm only stuck with him for a while and then Grant and I will be back together.

After lunch, I went to my locker to gather my books. Jack said he would meet me at the door but he wasn't there when I went. I looked out the window and saw Kendra backed up against Grant's car looking flushed and excited. I gritted my teeth together.

"I hate that girl!"

I jumped and turned around.

"The hell, Jack!" I yelled. He laughed.

"No, actually, it's just school, but close enough." I snorted and rolled my eyes.

"I can't believe this. They don't even seem fazed by seeing us," I said, shaking my head in disgust.

"I'm not surprised. It's going to take a little more than that for them to want us back."

I nodded and sighed. "I guess."

"Do I still have to come over to your house though?"

I looked at him and raised an eyebrow.

"Yes! What if someone sees you out? They'll know we are lying."

He grinned. "So you're really starting to enjoy this aren't you?"

"Yeah right!" I said and scoffed, turning so he couldn't see a little pink in my cheeks.

Jack took me back to my house and I got out of the rust bucket.

"It's not a rust bucket!" Jack said jumping out of the car. I looked at him and threw my head back and laughed.

"Yeah it is! Look at the bumper. It's about to fall off! And your mirror has a creak in it."

He pouted.

"You're not a very supportive girlfriend," he muttered. I shook my head.

"That's for school….not now." I unlocked the door and went in. He followed. I dropped my bag and took off the boots sighing with relief.

"Ha-ha!" he said and plopped himself down on the sofa. I rolled my eyes.

"This isn't your house! Get your feet off the sofa!" I growled. He laughed and kept them there, taunting me. I narrowed my eyes at him. "Jack, get them off. If my parents knew….they would slaughter you." He raised an eyebrow.

"What are you going to do about it, Princess? Claw me with your fingernails?"

"You little—!" I ran over there and grabbed his feet. He looked surprised. I threw them off but just as they went off he caught my arms and pulled at me.

"Freaking...tough...." He grunted, trying to get me down. I hit at his arm by flailing around my wrist. I then kicked him in the ribs with my foot playfully. I laughed and almost fell back. I tried to run but he caught my ankle and yanked me back and I landed on top of him. He grunted and I hit him in the chest.

"You're a tough one," he said. "And heavy!"

I gasped.

"Ass wipe!" I yelled. He laughed but grunted. I pushed at him and we both fell off the sofa. He was on me and I let out a huff.

"Yeah you are, too there, big boy! Now get off!" I yelled. I pushed at his arm and he laughed and then stopped as it gave out and he fell closer, his face now inches from mine. His deep blue eyes looked into mine and I swallowed. His body was warm above mine. His chest was tight and muscular and it tempted me. His lips were inches from mine and I kept looking at them. They looked so soft....my breathing was heavy and a piece of his hair touched my cheek. He looked really good....I felt....good. What is wrong with you?! Eww its Jack! I shook my head a little.

"Jack get off!" I yelled in his face. He frowned then jumped back.

"Gosh, you're such a prick," he said, laughing and shaking himself a little.

"Me? You're the one who wouldn't get your damn feet off my sofa!" I said giggling.

He laughed.

"I'm hungry," he said suddenly and went into the kitchen. I gave out a sigh and stood up. 'You've got to get yourself together Lidia! You're practically lusting over the first guy you have in sight since Grant. Get over yourself! Get a life! This is fake and it won't last long. So don't get used to it!' I went into the kitchen and Jack was drinking out of the milk carton.

"Hey!" I yelled. He smiled and a drip of milk slipped down his chin.

"Ah!" he said in delight and put it back in the fridge, wiping the back of his hand over his mouth.

"You're sick," I said and grabbed a granola bar from the cupboard. I sat on the counter and nibbled at it.

"Maybe we should go on a double date with them....well after a week or whatever. Just to show them that we're serious," I thought aloud.

"Yeah, we could do that," he said, shrugging. His hair came down in front of his eyes and he pushed it back. My stomach did flips...for some stupid reason! It was the granola bar! That's it. Yeah maybe I shouldn't have eaten it. It was making me feel sick.

"We should probably lay low for a while. Then when we see them, we act like the perfect couple," Jack said. I nodded. He moved his shoulder and winced. I grinned.

"My books are heavy aren't they?" I asked innocently. He glared daggers at me.

"You have no idea."

Chapter 6

One week later

One week later and we still hated each other. Probably more than the week before! Everyone asked us questions about dating and how we figured out we were so called 'in love'. We made up a lot as we went along. Jack was a total jerk to me! Outside of school that is. We fought like brother and sister.

"Honey!" Jack cooed coming to my locker. I smiled but I gritted my teeth together.

"Jacky!" I said nicknaming him. He glared for a moment then leaned against me on the locker. I hated when he did this!

"How was your day?" he asked. I pinched his side to get him off me but he just jumped and smirked.

"Fine, baby. Now, can we go home?" People were smiling and laughing at us.

"Nah, I thought I'd just leave you like this…it's much more relaxing."

"Ooh! Go Walker! He's got Taylor pinned on the locker!" one of his friends shouted. I smiled but it was forced. He saw and grinned. His leg was pinning my leg. Finally, I went for another attempt. I put my arms on his shoulder and grabbed his hair forcefully. He gave out a slight squeal but smiled.

"Lidia," he said.

"Kiss, kiss, kiss!" they chanted. He smirked.

"Not going to happen," I whispered and pulled at his hair.

"Ow, ow, ow," he whined.

"Let me go," he huffed and pulled back.

"Awe!"

I laughed.

"Let's go baby." I grabbed his arm and he squeezed it tightly. I winced and he smirked. See! We were always at each other's throat. We walked out of the school, Jack and me, trying to kill the other's hands.

"Hey!" Kendra said running over to us. I clenched my teeth.

"Hey," I managed to say. Grant smiled and waved from his car. I nodded. Ugh! They act like nothing's wrong! They don't even look the slightest bit jealous. This wasn't working!

"Do you guys want to go to the movies or something this weekend?" I looked at Jack who looked shocked for a second then regained himself.

"Sure, Kendra," he said calmly. She looked up at him and swallowed a little.

"O-oh okay," she stuttered. "Then we'll meet at the theater at 8 tomorrow night?" I nodded. She left quickly and I looked at Jack who gave me a smug look.

"What'd you do?" I asked. He looked down at me.

"I think she misses me."

I laughed and dropped his hand and headed towards his car.

"What? She was! She was looking all over me!"

I laughed again and we got in the car and started for my house.

"Are you staying?" I asked. He shook his head.

"No, I can't. My mom is having a friend over and she wants me to meet him."

I frowned. "Him? You never talk about your mom."

He shrugged.

"She's a great woman, my, mom. My dad left when I was about 10 so I took care of her. She dates every once in a while." His words were quiet and sad and somehow I respected him.

"That's nice," I said watching him.

He shrugged again. "Sure, I guess." I bit at my bottom lip.

"Actually, it really is," I said sincerely. He laughed.

"So, what now? You're going to go around telling people I'm some Momma's boy?" he snorted.

I frowned.

"No, I wouldn't do that." We made eye contact and we both froze. He quickly adjusted his eyes to the road.

"Thanks," he said quietly again. I nodded.

We got to my house and I saw my parents' car parked in the driveway.

"Oh crap, they're home." I mumbled. Jack laughed. We got out and walked to the front door. I went in and mom and dad were in the kitchen talking. "Mom? Dad?" I called.

"Oh sweetie!" Mom came running out, but stopped short as she saw me and Jack...and my different clothes. "You're a girl!" My mouth dropped and Jack burst out laughing.

"Yeah, mom I actually am. Thanks!" I yelled.

"Oh, I didn't mean it like that!" she said waving at me. She came over and gave me a big hug. "You look so pretty!" she gushed. My mom and I had the same hair color but hers was more like a bimbo. Fake boobs. Fake nails, fake hair extensions. I was the opposite of my mother. "Jack, it's a surprise to see you. Are Grant and Kendra coming over?" she asked. My heart dropped a little realizing she didn't know.

"Actually, Mom," I looked back at Jack who was speechless for once. He looked me in the eyes and nodded. "Grant and I broke up and now Jack and I are together." She raised an eyebrow.

"You're the Walker kid right?" my dad said from behind my mom. Jack nodded.

"Yes, sir," he extended a hand and my dad looked impressed for a moment. They shook hands.

"Awe, well that's sad, but don't worry Jack. We like you," said my mom, giving him a pinch with her fingers on his cheek and he grinned widely at me. I rolled my eyes and started for the stairs, not caring if he was coming or not. I went to my room and I heard him skipping up the stairs.

"Your mom is hot!" he said, coming in through my door. I turned to face him and let out a dramatic sigh.

"You would!" I said and shook my head.

"Your mom loves me!" he said and wiggled an eyebrow at me. "When we split up I'm going for her!" My mouth dropped and he came over and fell down onto my bed.

"Aren't you going to get together with Kendra?" I asked. He looked at me for a second, then looked away and shrugged. I hit his leg to move it and got my history book out from under it. "Don't you have to go home?" I asked and sat down. His leg hit my back and I rolled my eyes.

"Not right now. I want to annoy you more." I looked back at him. He had his arms crossed under his head and he grinned.

"Well, I'm going to bore you because I'm doing homework."

"You bore me anyhow."

I scrunched up my face and he laughed. I sighed and looked at my book while pulling off my sandals and throwing them in the corner. I pulled my hair back into a pony tail trying to get it out of my face and then started reading. "It's going to be weird tomorrow," Jack clarified.

"You think?" I muttered.

"I think we should make out during the movie."

I scoffed.

"Like I already told you, no! I'm not doing that!" I exclaimed.

He rolled his eyes at me.

"They aren't getting jealous or didn't you realize that?" he yelled.

"I know that! Maybe it's just because they are ok with it. Maybe we should just give it up." I sighed.

He rolled his eyes.

"You're so damn dramatic," he said, putting his fingers on the bridge of his nose.

"No, I'm being logical!"

He shook his head with his eyes closed.

"Well logic doesn't always work!" He opened his eyes and looked at me. They were blazing like a blue fire. My heart beat started going faster.

"F-fine," I said giving in. He looked surprised. "But I don't want to like make out, make out. Maybe just like kiss once or twice... Ewe I can't believe I just said that!"

He looked bored.

"Yeah, same here, but I want Kendra back." I looked at him and could see he was mad. Why would he be? But see, Lidia. He just wants her back. So just kiss him once or twice and you'll have Grant back. No worries.

"Ok, but don't like…" I tried to explain but I couldn't. He laughed.

"What? Don't what? I know how to kiss stupid. I'm probably better then you."

I gasped. "You're such a jerk! Probably not! I'll show you how to kiss, you little ass."

He raised an eyebrow but didn't object.

"Well, then, come on. Show me," he said getting comfortable on the bed.

"I don't think so—!"

"Dry lips?"

I gritted my teeth together.

"Fine!" I dropped my books to the floor and got on the bed. I straddled him and his eyes got wide. I smirked.

"This is how you kiss," I leaned down and he stared up at me. I can't believe I'm doing this! Get a hold of yourself, Lidia! Get off him and tell him you're done with this whole fake relationship! But I couldn't. His lips looked so soft and sweet. I leaned down and he lifted his head a little. Our lips touched softly and my stomach did flips. They were soft. I forced open his lips and sucked on his top lip. Now this was showing him! His hands wrapped themselves around my waist holding me closer. They were burning me. His lips, his hands….a moan almost escaped my mouth but I held it in. He tasted of peppermint and cigarettes. I didn't want to end the kiss and I could tell that he didn't want to either. I was quickly losing my breath and my head was getting foggy. I really wanted to take off—.

"Honey I was—."

I jumped back and stared at my mother at the door. Her eyes were wide, then she smiled. "Oh, I'm sorry sweetie." I looked down at Jack and he grinned up at me, his hands closer to my butt. I slapped his hands and got off him.

"No, Mom, it's not what you think."

"No, no, it's okay honey."

I shook my head with my eyes wide.

"No I was just…he was….Jack, go home!" I finally yelled turning around to him. He laughed and sat up.

"She just can't think right after we kiss. I'm glad I have that effect on her."

I glared at him as he picked up his jacket and backpack.

"Sorry, Mrs. Taylor," he said sweetly. He looked at me, winked then smiled at my mom. "Bye!" he ran out the door and down stairs. My mom chuckled.

"He really is a sweet boy. I hope you're being safe, too."

I stared at her my mouth open. "Mom! I'm not having sex!"

She sighed. "Honey, a mother knows when her daughter is."

"Mom, please, you don't know anything about me."

She frowned. "Lidia I—."

"I have homework."

She stopped, nodded and then left. I shut the door. His car pulled away from my driveway and went down the road. I sighed and laid back on the bed. My pillow had a dent in the top and I smelled it. The aroma was a bittersweet cologne. Jack's. I licked my lips and still tasted him. Get a hold of yourself, girl! With that, I put the pillow back and started my homework.

Chapter 7

Saturday. One of the best days of the week. No school, just sleep and do nothing. Peaceful sleep. Something I hadn't gotten in a while. Just peace.

"Yo, Taylor! Get up!" I jumped and flipped around in bed to frown at Jack. He looked at me, raised an eyebrow then laughed.

"Get out!" I yelled. "And who the hell let you in?" He laughed again.

"Your mom did," he winked. "And she told me to tell you that it's 3:30 p.m. and that they're leaving to go out to dinner and visit some friends." I rolled my eyes.

"Thanks. Now, get out." I shoved my face back into the pillow, wanting more sleep.

"Gosh, how many hours do you need, Princess?" he muttered. I threw an arm up at him to silence him and he got quiet. I sighed. I felt the bed squeak as someone sat down. I didn't care, I was so tired. It might have been my mind playing tricks on me but I swore I felt someone stroking my hair; then pushing it away from my face, his fingers rough but gentle. Yeah, I was definitely dreaming!

His blonde hair blew across his face, his perfect smile glistening in the sunlight. "Grant?" I asked, surprised. He stood in front of me. "Hey," he said and smiled. I frowned. "I wanted to tell you something." I shifted my feet. "Yeah?" I asked, my heart pounding. "I want you back. I'm in love with you." I smiled. "Really?" He nodded and got down on his knees. "Lidia I can't live without you. I want you back. I love you so much," he was begging. I laughed and nodded. "Yes! I…"

I groaned. No! I couldn't finish it! I felt something hard under me. It was breathing. What? Breathing? I looked up and I was laying half way on Jack. His eyes were closed. His hand was on my back, our legs tangled together. My eyes widened. Holy cow! I looked at the clock and saw it was 7:00 pm.

"Oh, shoot!" I yelled. Jack jumped up and almost smashed heads with mine.

"For the love of God, Lidia!" he yelled. I looked at him then jumped off of him and shook myself.

"Ewe, ewe, ewe! That was sick! Why would you do that? Ewe! I got Jack coodies!" I yelled, feeling not even the slightest bit dirty, but I wanted him to think I did. He laughed.

"Me? You think I did that? Princess, you cuddled up to me first!" My mouth dropped.

"I..did not! You're lying!"

He shrugged and looked at me with the corner of his eye. It was the truth. I clenched my teeth. "Ugh, would you get off my bed?! You're making it dirty! I'll be back. I'm going to take a shower." I grabbed my clothes and hurried to the bathroom, locking the door. I breathed deeply. I can't believe I did that! I don't remember cuddling up to him. But he didn't look mad..he actually looked...I gulped. Happy or pleased.

After my shower, I changed into a short skirt and a pretty dark purple top, blow dried my hair and did my makeup. I went back into the room and Jack was still lying on my bed with his eyes closed. I didn't want to wake him but then I wanted to jump up on the bed and scare the crap out of him. I put my clothes in my hamper and bent down to pick up an earring that had fallen.

"You have a great ass, did anyone ever tell you that?" I jumped and turned around. Jack was watching me. His hands behind his head, his hair sweeping down in front of his eyes. I rolled my eyes.

"No, but thanks," I said sarcastically. "Get up. We need to go," I ordered. He sighed and got up. He ran his hand through his hair once and then put on his shoes. I turned around and grabbed a pair of high-heeled sandals and sat in my desk chair to put them on. "Do we have an escape plan?" I asked. Jack laughed as he tied his shoe.

"I don't know. We could say that your parents need you back home by a certain time."

I nodded.

"Sounds good to me." We both got up at the same time. I looked him up and down. He was wearing a nice pair of dark jeans with an ivory shirt plus his black leather jacket. I snorted then got my purse. This was going to be an interesting night.

Chapter 8

"No! Stop it!" Jack yelled at me. I growled.

"It hurts that way!" I grabbed his hand and put our fingers together then made sure my arm was over his. Because the other way my arm got cramps. And he knew that. We were walking to the movie theater, still fighting. "Jack! Cut it out!" I yelled. He smirked. I grabbed the back of his head with a fist full of hair.

"Ow!" he yelled and grabbed mine.

"Let go," I warned and pulled harder. He grunted.

"Not till you do," and he pulled just as hard. I whimpered.

"Fine!" I finally let go and then he did, too. I held the back of my head and rubbed it. He did the same. "You're such a girl," I muttered.

He shook his head.

"You're such a boy."

I scowled at him. We went to the ticket counter, no longer holding hands and got our tickets, continuing to argue. "Look, there they are," he whispered. Grant and Kendra stood by the entrance to the movie, gazing into each other's eyes. Grant had never looked at me that way before. My heart sank. Were they really in love? Did we even have a chance to get back together with them? I glanced over at Jack and could see that the same questions were running in his mind. I took his hand the way he wanted it but didn't look at him. His fingers wrapped around mine gently. We walked over and put on our best smiles.

"Hey guys!" I called. They turned towards us and smiled. Grant put his arm around Kendra and she put hers around him. I tried to ignore the sudden urge to frown. Grant looked at me with his eyes a little wide. I stood next to Jack smiling. He gulped.

"Aw, I hope I don't get scared," Kendra said to Grant holding on and laughing a little. I heard Jack snort but they, thankfully, didn't hear him.

"I know!" I agreed and held onto Jack's arm. He looked down at me and gave me a wink and a smile.

"It's okay, baby. I'll take care of you," he said flirtatiously. I smiled and batted my eye lashes.

"Lidia, you've always loved scary movies. You were never scared of them before," Grant said with a small laugh. I looked at him and glared.

"I've changed a lot since then Grant." He cleared his throat and I looked back at Jack. He rolled his eyes. I shrugged and we went into the theater. The credits were playing and there were only about a dozen people in the place. We went to the third row from the top and sat down. Kendra sat beside me with Jack on my other side. My hands were sweating. As soon as we settled down, Jack and I let our hands go. Sometimes it was awkward with him. I put my feet up on the chair in front of me and Jack did the same. The movie started and I took in a deep breath. So, this isn't too bad. It felt like old times, when we would go out together. Kendra and I would sit like this. It's just that this time, Jack was with me and Grant was with her. See, no differences. I smiled lightly. I looked down and saw Jack's hand on the arm rest. It was long and thin. His fingers looked rough but I knew how gentle and soft they were. Did Kendra know this? Or did she just go out with him because whatever? I heard a giggle after someone screamed in the movie and looked over. Grant was nuzzling Kendra's neck whispering something. I gritted my teeth together. I looked over at Jack who looked bored but kept looking at the screen.

"Jack?" I whispered and pinched his arm. He looked over at me and sighed. "Kiss me." His eyes widened from what I could see.

"What?" he asked.

"I said, kiss me." My breath was low. He looked around me and saw Kendra and Grant. He narrowed his eyes at them then turned to me. He surprised me by putting his hand on my jaw and bringing me closer to him. His hand was cold on my neck, but I liked it. I made the first move and kissed him. His lips were warm and just the way they felt yesterday but more....I wasn't sure. My stomach was fluttering with butterflies and I felt like I was floating. It sure didn't feel this way with Grant! But why didn't it? We parted our lips and tongues touched. I gasped a little but put my hands in his hair. His other hand was on my shoulder. Our breathing was heavy and we had to pull back before we couldn't breathe at all. I bit at my lip as we looked at each other. I didn't know what to say. We both felt like it was different for each other. I could tell. But I wasn't going to admit that.

"I think they saw, so that's all we'll do," I said, trying not to sound frazzled. He nodded stiffly and we turned back to the movie.

Chapter 9

"Wow! That was such a good movie!" Kendra gushed as we went back to our cars. I looked over at her and raised an eyebrow.

"Do you even know what it was about?" I asked. She stared at me for a moment, looking like a blow-up doll.

"Um, yeah!" She looked away. She didn't even know. It was a good movie, but it wasn't scary.

"So, you guys want to go to the Burger restaurant?" asked Kendra. I looked at Jack and shrugged.

"Sure, Kendra," he said and put his hand around my waist. It surprised me.

"My baby needs something to eat." I looked over at her nervously. She smiled, but it quivered.

"Y-yeah of course," she stuttered. We got back into our cars and went to the restaurant.

"Well, that turned out pretty well," I mumbled, as we headed to the door and went in. Kendra and Grant followed slowly behind us. Jack laughed.

"Yeah, sure it did. Like it wasn't awkward or weird at all."

We reached the restaurant soon after. He opened the door for me and I went in. He held it open for Grant and Kendra. I smiled at him. He came back beside me and Grant and Kendra found a seat in the corner. Jack slid in first and then I went in beside him. Grant and Kendra sat across from us. The place was busy and I figured we wouldn't be served for a while.

"So how are you two doing?" Kendra asked leaning over the table to us. She sat across from Jack. Grant watched me and I tried not to look at him. Jack sighed and laid a lazy arm around my shoulder. I smiled.

"Great! I just love my Jacky!" I said and playfully knocking him in the side. He grinned. It felt weird doing this. I hated being fake and plastic. But this is how I was going to make Grant jealous.

"Yeah, and I love you too," he pinched my cheek and I tried to smile but it came out forced. He saw and grinned wider.

"Aww, you're just so cute!" I said.

"Not as cute as you!" he said.

"Well I have to give you that one!" I wiggled my eye brows and he glared for a moment but then smiled. "So, yeah we're doing great!" Kendra smiled but it wasn't real. I saw it before. Grant looked mad but then Kendra put her hand on his lap and patted it.

"We are, too!" she had expected us to ask but we hadn't. She sighed.

"Hello, how may I help you?" asked a waitress.

"Oh yeah!" Jack slapped my butt and winked at Grant. Grant merely smiled. I laughed and turned to glare at him.

"Jack get out so I can sit down." I said and smiled. He grinned and stood up.

"I'll be right back," Jack said and headed to the restroom. Kendra did the same. I sat back down in the seat and wished I had gone too. This was really awkward.

"So you and Walker," Grant said nodding. I nodded. This was the first time I had been alone with him since we'd broke up. "You really like him?" he asked. I looked up and narrowed my eyes at him.

"Yeah, I do." He clenched his teeth.

"I was thinking…" he said looking down. "I thought maybe we could—. "

"Back! Did ya miss me?" Jack said with a grin and his arms open. I smiled.

"Of course!" I giggled and he slid in next to me. Kendra came back and looked at Grant. "My mom said I need to be home in 10 minutes. So let's go." Grant stood up hastily and put his jacket back on.

"Awe, ok," I said and pushed Jack to stand up.

"Yeah, sorry," she said quickly. Jack smirked.

"OK well, bye," I said and waved. She waved but frowned. Both of them walked out and we watched them get into their car and drive away. What was Grant going to tell me? Jack, gently starting gliding his hand down to my butt. I slapped it and threw it back at him and then went out the door.

"Aw, come on!" he complained. I rolled my eyes and got into his car.

Chapter 10

About a month later

One whole month and a week later, Jack and I were still trying our best to make Grant and Kendra jealous; but it didn't matter what we did, nothing seemed to bother them. Once in a while they would break but then they would act as if nothing happened. But we weren't giving up. Jack and I would still rant on to each other and fight but it was better. But, we hadn't kissed since that night.

"Oh, would you just shut up!" Jack complained as we entered my house.

"You shut up! I'm the one who has to deal with you!" I yelled. He threw himself down on the sofa dramatically. "Drama queen," I muttered. He grinned.

"Get me something to eat," he ordered, grabbing the TV remote.

"What do I look like? Your slave?" I questioned, putting my hands on my hips. He looked me up and down and was about to say something but I put a finger up. "Just don't answer that." He laughed. I went upstairs to change out of my tight clothes and put on a pair of my loose jeans and a tank top. I put my hair up in a ponytail and went back downstairs. I cooked grilled cheese and got two beers from the fridge. My parents wouldn't be home till late, so why not? I went back into the living room and slapped his plate down onto the coffee table. He looked up at me with his eyes wide. "What?" I asked frowning. I pushed his feet and sat down. He kept looking at me strangely.

"Oh...nothing," he forced his eyes away from me and I kept frowning as I bit into my sandwich. I handed him a beer and he raised an eyebrow. I shrugged and opened mine. It tasted awful but I really didn't care. We were watching an old rerun of Smallville. I loved the show.

"So, you watch this?" I asked taking another swig of my drink. He nodded.

"Yeah, it's cool."

Five beers, 4 episodes of Smallville and 4 hours later and we were loopy. "Oh my gosh! I can't believe Chloe would reject him like that!" I yelled as my hands flopped by my sides. Jack and I were lounged on the sofa with our heads almost touching and our bodies hanging slouching.

"But Clark was being an ass! He deserved it." I rolled my eyes.

"But she is his friend she should be okay with whatever Clark decides." Jack sighed.

"It's just the way it is," he said. I frowned. Our words had slurred halfway through our second beer. Wow, who knew you could get buzzed off of that! It was dark out and I didn't know when my parents would be home. Jack blew out a breath and I looked over at him. My mind was foggy again. My body over took me before I could even control it. I sat on my knees and looked down at Jack. He looked up at me then saw something in my eyes. His eyes got serious for a moment then turned drunkenly happy. He grabbed my waist and yanked me down on top of him. I gave out a shriek giggle and started kissing him. Our legs got tangled together and I ran my hands through his hair. I didn't care if I was drunk! This was good! And even though I didn't exactly feel drunk, he didn't know that. So the next day, if he asked why I kissed him I would say I was drunk, not that I actually might have feelings for him and wanted to kiss him so badly. And he was, too. So he'd think we both were and didn't mean to. Yes, it was perfect! And he was drunk. The way he was holding me, the way he was kissing me, was like nothing before! He was definitely drunk! Our tongues came together and I moaned. He kissed my neck and I smiled, my eyes closed. Man, this felt so good! I was hot. He kissed down my throat to the middle of my chest where a freckle was. He kissed it and I felt lust for him. Or more than that? Then his phone vibrated. We both jumped and he pushed me off him. I grumbled and stood up. He grabbed his phone, wiping his mouth with the back of his hand.

"Yeah?" he asked out of breath. "Mom!...yeah...what's wrong..?" Worry started to build in my stomach. He clenched his teeth. "Yeah, I'll be there…it's okay...yeah I'm coming home." He stood up and looked at me while putting his shoes on. "Listen, I got to go." His words were crisp and clear.

"Why? Is something wrong?" I asked. He shook his head.

"No. Well, I'm not sure. But I have to go." He wobbled a little.

"Wait, should you really be driving?" He half smiled at me.

"Yeah I'm fine." I nodded. He came over to me and stared down into my eyes. "Bye," he said and then left. I heard his car start up and blew out a quivering breath. 'Wow that was exciting!' I thought. 'But wait. You don't like him, remember?' I reminded myself.

"Yeah, I don't like him. I'm just using him," I thought and smiled.

"Lidia?" I was in my room doing homework that night when my mom called. I went down the stairs and she was in the kitchen holding empty beer cans.

"Mom, I-I-I...I can explain," I stuttered. I'd forgotten to get rid of the cans! Ugh! Why was I so silly? She shook her head.

"How many did you drink?" she asked.

"Just five and Jack had five too." She sighed and closed her eyes.

"Lidia, I'm disappointed, but I'm not going to ground you." I looked at her surprised.

51

"What? Why?" She laughed and then smiled.

"They're non-alcoholic, sweetie." My mouth fell to the ground as she came over to me and kissed my forehead. "Night." I swear a fly went into my mouth. If I wasn't drunk…and he wasn't drunk...and we were both sober...that means...I gulped. We both did that. We both wanted to make out with each other.

"Non-alcoholic beer...what the—."

Chapter 11

The next day Jack didn't call or come over. He didn't pick my calls up on Monday morning either. I was almost late for school when I arrived just before the bell rang. I sighed loudly as I ran into class. Jack wasn't there. I frowned wondering what was wrong. Should I text him? Maybe he decided that he didn't want get back together with Kendra and just decided to give up. I sat down in the back row and stared off into space.

I saw Jack moving in the crowd but I couldn't get to him so I went to his locker and there he was.

"Jack!" I said angrily. He looked over at me with a blank expression on his face. "What happened? You said you were going to pick me up today." He looked at me with a frown on his face then turned back to his locker. "Jack?" I whispered. He didn't look at me. "Would you look at me, please?" I yelled, grabbing his arm. He turned around and his eyes were dark blue. No emotions in them. "What happened on Saturday night?" I asked. "Is your mom okay?" I asked, really worried. He looked away and then back at me.

"Why the hell do you care?" he said. I was so stunned that I didn't even move. He pushed past me and went in through to the crowd without a glance back at me.

"Aw, are you two having a rough patch?" Kendra asked, coming to my side. She had a little compassion on her face and I ignored the urge to punch her. I put on a fake smile.

"Not really. It's just that he's in a crappy mood. You know how guys get." She nodded, looking mad by my cheeriness.

"One thing you got to know about Jack is that he can be bipolar." She acted as if she knew him more than me. Which she did but I was turned off with her acting that way.

"Oh really? Wow, he has never been that way to me before!" I said, acting stunned. She glared. "He's always so happy with me. Maybe it was just something he got over when we got together." She was now glaring daggers at me.

"Well maybe—." she started, but Grant came up behind her and put his hand around her waist.

"Hey Lidia," said Grant, smirking at me.

"Hi," I said biting the inside of my mouth.

"Oh, Grant. It was horrible. Jack is completely being a jerk and totally blew her off. I really hope you two don't break up." She fluttered her eye lashes and pouted. This time I glared.

"No, we're not breaking up. We're just in a bad place today."

Grant shrugged.

"Well, if you need anything, ask. We're always here if Jack blows you off again." I wanted to rip both of their heads off.

"Yeah, okay," I said and walked away. Damn them! I hated them! Oh but Jack was so dead! I didn't want to talk to him at all that day! He was being an asshole!

The last bell rang and I quickly went to my locker trying not to let anyone see that I was alone. Kendra was probably already spreading rumors about Jack and me.

"Hey Lidia!" I turned around and saw my other friend Candice running over with my history book. "Here. You left this in there."

"Oh, thanks!" I said relieved. "Wow, I can't believe I almost forgot that!" She laughed.

"Big test tomorrow, too." I nodded and groaned. "I hate tests."

"You and me, both!" We laughed together. "Hey, are you going to try out for the play?"

I laughed.

"No, I don't think so."

"Aw, you should. It's Hamlet and I'm producing it."

"Oh, that's cool!" I said.

"Lidia," I turned around and saw Jack making his way through to us. I looked back at Candice.

"Ugh, sorry. I should probably go." She smiled.

"It's fine. We can talk in History." I nodded.

"Thanks again for the book!"

She nodded and I took off down the hall.

"Lidia!" he yelled. I didn't turn around. If he could run away, so could I! "Would you stop?!" he yelled. People were watching us. I got to the door and was about to open it when he grabbed my arm, swinging me around.

"Let go!" I threatened.

"Would you stop? I'm trying to talk to you!" he whispered fiercely. I rolled my eyes. "Whatever you have to say, you can save your breath." I pulled my arm back.

"Listen, I'm sorry!" he said rolling his eyes. I shook my head.

"You left me. Grant and Kendra completely humiliated me! No thanks to you!" I gritted my teeth together. He shook his head clenching his teeth. "See, that's what I thought." I swung open the door accidentally hitting him in the stomach with it. I didn't turn back, I just went out to my jeep.

"Ugh! You are such a pain in the ass, you know that?" Jack said running behind me. I ignored him. I put my bag in the back and got into my car. "Lidia, come on," he said pleading. I looked at him through the window. His eyes were sad. 'No, Lidia. Don't you dare! He was a jerk to you. You don't need that foolishness from him.' I looked away and drove off.

"Lidia! There you are," my mom said, as I came in through the door. I raised an eyebrow at her. "What?" She smiled.

"Now, now don't say anything. Just let me tell you. Okay, so there is this Beauty Pageant in New York this weekend and I—"

"No!" I yelled rolling my eyes. She frowned.

"But honey it's—"

"I said no. How many times do we have to go through this, Mom? I don't want to do that! I don't want to do what you did." She pouted.

"I got a couple of scholarships to really good colleges. You—"

"Yeah, and you didn't even go to any of them." She huffed.

"I just want what's best for you sweetie." She came over and put her hands on my face.

"Then let me do what I want."

She scrunched her nose.

"What was it that you wanted to do?"

I rolled my eyes, pushed her hands away from me and walked around her.

"I want to go to medical school to become a doctor."

She put her hands on her hips and turned around to face me.

"Oh…that," she sounded disgusted. I ignored it. I wasn't in the mood.

"Where's Dad?" I asked. Her eyes looked hurt for a moment.

"Um, he's with, um a meeting at his work."

I nodded. "I'm going upstairs."

She nodded. I went to my room and changed into comfortable clothes. I hated wearing this uncomfortable stuff. The tight jeans, the tight reveling shirts, the high heels. I hated not being myself anymore. I forgot how much I liked being myself.

Chapter 12

That morning I neither put on a lot of makeup nor wear the fancy shirts. Instead, I wore a pair of nice dark jeans and one of my old T-shirts. I slipped on my jacket and grabbed my backpack. Mom was downstairs making breakfast, which surprised me because she couldn't really cook.

"Hey baby, I made pancakes." I frowned at her.

"I can't eat. I have to go."

She sighed. She had powder on her nose from the mix and she looked very tired. "Are you okay?" I asked. She smiled and nodded.

"Yeah, I'm fine. Have a good day at school." I nodded, still a little worried. As I got my keys out of my purse and opened the front door Jack was already there leaning on his car. I jumped when I saw him, very surprised.

"Ready?" he asked. I didn't speak one word to him. I almost ran to my jeep. He caught me. "I don't think so!" he said laughing a little. I grunted and tried to get him to let me go. "You're coming with me!" he said and pulled me by my waist away from my car. I struggled and struggled, but he had too much of a good grip on me.

"Ugh, put me down!" I yelled. He laughed.

"No!" He dragged me over to his car and started to open the passenger's side. I kneed him in the stomach. He reacted and I quickly got out from under his arm but that wasn't enough time. He spun and grabbed me and put me over his shoulder.

"Man, you're heavy," he complained. I hit him in the back and he winced. He dunked me down and tried putting me in the car but I stuck my arm out and caught the top of the car. "Just get in the car!" he yelled. I laughed and pushed myself back out but he pushed me in. We both were laughing at this point.

"Hey! Is something wrong?" We both jumped and I looked up to see our neighbor looking at us strangely.

"Um, no, Mr. Rogers I'm fine." He nodded and went back to his yard work, still feeling suspicious. Jack looked back at me his eyes amused.

"You have a neighbor named Mr. Rogers?" At that point I burst out laughing, nodding my head. He laughed, too. I was lying on the seat on my back as my legs were wrapped around one of his legs. It was a very weird way to sit, but it was funny. "Can we just go to school?" he asked sighing. I smiled and nodded. I let go of him and he let go of me. I turned myself around in the seat and he got in though the other side.

"You know that I totally would have won!"

He laughed and shook his head. "No way! You were so weak!"

"Says my knee to your stomach!" he rubbed his stomach and pouted. I laughed.

"Whatever. That's what you think."

"It is," I smirked and he playfully glared.

"So, are you guys ok now?" Kendra asked, coming up to our table during lunch. Jack narrowed his eyes at her. He reached across the table and put his hand over mine.

"Yeah, we're fine now. Actually we're more than fine." He gave me a smile that almost made me stop breathing. Wow, he was really good at faking! Something in me wished he wasn't. Kendra bit her lip roughly.

"That's good," she said. Grant smiled at me but I rolled my eyes.

"Hey!" Candice said coming up to our table. I smiled.

"Hey, Candice. How did you do on the test?" She sighed and sat down on a chair beside me with her lunch.

"I think I did well. But who knows? What about you?"

Kendra was completely ignored and she and Grant retreated.

"I have no idea. But if I fail this, I'm dead meat!" Jack laughed.

"Oh, Candice, this is Jack," I introduced. She smiled kindly at him.

"Hi, Candice," he said and shook her hand. She seemed impressed.

"Do you know Tommy Collins?" she asked. He thought for a moment.

"Yeah, he's in gym with me. He's a cool guy."

She grinned.

"He's my boyfriend."

He smiled.

"Well, he's a lucky man then." I bit my lip as I watched him talking to her like a normal, kind guy. He was sweet. How come I never saw this side of him before? I looked down at my tray of half eaten food and blushed.

"Lidia?" I looked up. Jack looked amused and Candice just smiled. "You okay?" I nodded eagerly.

"Yeah I'm great." But will I be great when this thing with Jack is over?

"So, you and Jack," Candice said as we walked to English. I nodded.

"Yeah after Grant broke up with me Jack asked me out. I said yes." The way I said it, it sounded so reread. She saw it too and raised an eyebrow.

"Interesting."

I nodded and looked away from her. "Well, you guys are cute together. I think you, Jack, Tommy and I should go out together. It would be fun." I smiled over at her.

"That would be fun." Wait, what are you doing Lidia? You're with Jack to make Grant jealous, not to actually go on double dates with other people! But would it really hurt?

"Tommy would love Jack. But my parents don't like Tommy. They think he's a bad influence on me."

I laughed. "But he's sweet and so what if he smokes? He's a great guy." I smiled at her. She looked like she was glowing when she talked about him. She looked at me. "I see the way Jack looks at you." I clenched my teeth. Her eyes were soft. "He looks at you as if you're the sun itself in the sky. It's really romantic." Her words drowned in my ears. Was that for show too? Did he really look at me that way? Why would he? This whole relationship was fake! How could he do that? Questions swarmed in my head that needed answers.

"H-he...really?" I asked, my mouth going dry. She smiled and nodded.

"You guys are really meant for each other." There was a giant lump in my throat that I couldn't swallow.

"Thanks, Candice," I said. She nodded and went on talking about something else. I looked down the hall but I wasn't really seeing anything. Why was he looking at me like that?

Chapter 13

I felt distant at school. I just didn't feel like myself. Jack asked if I wanted him to stay, but as much as I wanted him to, I needed space. So I said I was just going to study. He nodded, but seemed suspicious and left. I watched him get back into his car and drive away. After changing my clothes, I went out the back door, across my yard and Mr. Rogers' yard to one of my favorite spots. I needed air. I needed to get my head straight. I couldn't get Candice's conversation out of my head.

"I see the way Jack looks at you. He looks at you as if you're the sun itself in the sky. It's really romantic..." It echoed in my ears. 'It was fake, remember, Lidia? He's just a really good actor. He's good at faking it. The looks, the smiles, the way he seems protective when Grant comes around...It's all fake.' I opened up the old rusty gate and walked in my little playground. I went to my swing and sat down. The air was cold, warning us that winter was coming. Even though it was freezing, I took off my shoes and ran my feet through the sand beneath me. I sighed and started to swing. Other things were on my mind, too. Things that I should be worrying about. My head started to hurt and I brought the swing to a slow back and forth. The thing squeaked every time I went back.

"I knew I'd find you in here." I jumped slightly and looked up, startled. Jack stood at the gate and smiled at me. His blue eyes looked lighter and kinder today. My heartbeat went faster.

"Um, yeah," I said and looked down. Part of me wanted to scream at him to go away and leave me alone. The other part wanted him to hold me. Huh…why? He sighed and came over to me. He sat in the swing next to mine and started moving.

"Are you going to tell me what's on your mind?" he asked, kicking his feet up in the air. I couldn't! I couldn't ask him why he would look at me...look at me in a way you would only look at someone….someone like your real girlfriend. Someone you really loved. It would be so humiliating if he said it was just for show. I would embarrass myself too much. I looked over at him and he was wearing his leather jacket but a pack of cigarettes were in it. "Since when do you smoke?" I asked. He slowed to a stop and grabbed it out of his pocket. He shrugged.

"Only once in a while. When I'm stressed. My friend buys them for me." I nodded and he stuck them back into his pocket. "You got off the subject," he said looking at me with a half-smile. I looked down at my hands and started to move my feet.

"It's nothing."

He groaned. "Would you look at me?"

I wouldn't.

"Olli—."

Before I knew it I was spitting out something else.

"My dad's cheating on my mom," I said, cutting him off. The words I had spoken hurt me deeper than I thought they would.

"What?" Jack asked, confused.

"I never wanted to admit it. But two years ago I followed him to work. He didn't go to work. He went to a prostitute house…I think my mom knows now." It was silent. The only sound was the wind blowing the dead leaves.

"Oh," Jack said quietly. I rubbed my fingers together.

"I was going to tell her but I couldn't. It would break her." I saw him nod.

"Lidia," he said and the word made a shiver run down my spine. I finally looked over at him. "I don't know how you're feeling but I can understand somehow." I searched his face for something that would indicate he was just messing with my head. That he didn't care. But it was the opposite. His eyes were soft, sad and understanding.

"How?" I asked. His eyes glazed over a little.

"When my dad left, he had a whole other family in California. He had another wife and 5 children. My mom was the other woman." My mouth fell a little. "She got pregnant with me and my dad stayed here for a while then he decided he didn't want us anymore and went back to his old wife." His teeth were clenched, his hands in fist. Finally he came out of his thoughts and looked at me. His eyes were a little shocked that he had told me all of that. "See, we're not so different, are we?"

I smiled lightly.

"No, I guess not." I looked away but that wasn't the big thing on my mind. He didn't even know it was about him.

"Cold out here, isn't it?" he asked, shrugging.

I nodded. "A little."

"Here," he slipped off his leather jacket and gave it to me.

"Jack, you don't have to," I said, shaking my head. He just smiled and put it around my shoulders.

"You might be my fake girlfriend but I guess you can wear it," he winked and sat back down on his swing.

I laughed. "Thanks."

He nodded and smiled. He was wearing a long sleeved navy blue shirt but he didn't look the slightest bit cold. Then I saw something I hadn't seen before. A bruise on his shoulder. I frowned. Why would he have a bruise that big on his shoulder? I never saw that before. I didn't comment. "It's getting late," I said. He kept on swinging.

"I don't want to go home." he said like a stubborn kid. I laughed. But he was serious.

"Is something wrong?" I asked, concerned.

He shook his head and looked over at me softly.

"No."

I was still frowning. I stopped my swing and stood up. He stopped too. I stood in front of him and leaned down. He watched my eyes. I closed my eyes and kissed his cheek. It was soft and warm. Then slowly I slid my lips across his cheek to his lips. He didn't move but I could feel his breathing pick up. I gently kissed him then pulled back. His eyes opened and he had something strange in them. He had some kind of deep emotion in them.

"Thanks," I whispered, smiling. He nodded but stayed quiet. I gave him back his jacket and then left the playground. For some reason, my body wanted to go back to him but I had to get home. I had to talk to my mom. I touched my lips and still felt the warmth from him there.

Chapter 14

I had talked to my mom about stuff. She and I were a lot more alike than I'd thought. We didn't talk about dad or anything though, because anytime I tried to bring it up she would push it away, because she felt uncomfortable talking about it. We fell asleep in her room with her arms around me. It was nice. I felt like I was 5 years old again, sleeping with mommy.

A couple of days passed by and nothing really happened. On Wednesday morning, I got up late, quickly showered and got dressed.

"Honey, don't forget your money!" Mom yelled from the kitchen. She said that dad would be back by Friday sometime. But that's all she said. I didn't know what was happening to my parents. I didn't know what was in the future for our family but I was sure I wasn't taking my father's side.

There was a knock on the door and I answered it while slipping on my jacket. Jack looked good but something was annoying about him.

"Hold on," I said and went to my mom in the kitchen. "Bye, Mom," I kissed her cheek and she smiled.

"Bye, honey. Oh, I'm going to Sue's this evening, so I won't be home." I nodded, grabbed my bag and ran out past Jack and into his car.

"What's wrong with you?" he asked as he got into the car. I looked at him and frowned.

"I'm fine. What's wrong with you?" I asked. He raised an eyebrow.

"Women," he muttered shaking his head.

I don't know why I was mad. I just was. I was mad because Jack acted as if everything was okay. I was mad that he let me kiss him. I was mad that he didn't care about me like I think I did for him. He was just making fun of me, I think. "You want to sit with us?" I asked Candice during recess. She smiled.

"Sure." We sat at our usual table. Kendra and Grant hadn't sat with us for a while but other friends of ours sat at the lower end of the table. Jack sat down next to me putting an arm around my shoulder. I looked over at him and he grinned.

"I wonder where Tommy is." Candice looked around and that's when I threw Jack's arm off. "Ouch!" Candice looked back at us and we smiled. She frowned slightly.

"Hey," Tommy said as he kissed Candice on the head and smiled.

"Tommy, this is Jack and Lidia. Remember, I told you about them."

"Yeah!" he smiled. He was a big, tall boy with blonde hair and brown eyes. Quite handsome. "Hey, man!" he said and slapped hands with Jack.

"How's it going?" Jack asked already enthralled with talking about stupid boy stuff. Candice sighed and I laughed a little.

"So, how's the play going?" I asked her. She smiled.

"Great! It's going great! I still think you should try out."

I snorted.

"I don't think acting is my thing."

Jack looked over at me, his lips twitching a little.

"Babe, I think you're a good actress." I narrowed my eyes at him.

"Really? You know, I just can't see myself like that. Though you, you would be perfect for the jackass costume but you wouldn't—. "

"Ha-ha!" he said cutting me off. I smirked. Candice and Tommy were laughing. Jack glared. "Sorry baby, just helping." I pouted and he looked annoyed for a moment and then continued talking to Tommy. Candice laughed.

"Oh! Hey do you guys still want to go out on a double date?" She asked Jack and me.

"Um, Candice I don't—"

"Yeah that would be great!" Jack said cutting in once again. I looked over at him clenching my teeth. He put his arm around me and it took everything not to hit him. Candice grinned.

"Awesome! It'll be fun. You guys just want to get together and watch movies and have popcorn and stuff?" she asked. Jack nodded before I could say anything. "So maybe like Friday night after school?"

"Sure," I said sounding sarcastic.

"Um, Tommy do you have a big TV?" she asked. He took a big bite of his sandwich and looked over at her.

"It's not that big," he said with his mouth full. She rolled her eyes.

"We can have it at Lidia's. She has a big TV and I'm sure Mr. and Mrs. Taylor won't mind," offered Jack. I grabbed his leg and squeezed. He jumped and breathed in.

"Oh, okay, cool! Is that okay, Lidia?" she asked, sounding sweet. I nodded.

"Yeah, that's fine," I was still grabbing his leg and gripping it hard. He groaned a little and squeezed my shoulder. I jerked my head to the side as he pinched a pressure point. Candice and Tommy were talking, not bothering to see us fighting, thankfully.

"Jack!" I yelled quietly. He was gritting his teeth together.

"Let go," he said. I did and he did, too. We both exhaled and rubbed where the other person had hurt us. I glared at him.

"We're talking about this when we get to my house!"

"Nuew," he said shaking his head, making fun of me.

"I can't stand you!" I yelled in his ear. He snorted. I stood up and took my tray to throw out the leftovers.

"Damn it, Jack!" I yelled as we got into my house. He dropped his stuff by the door like me. "What?" he yelled throwing his hands in the air. I threw my coat on the sofa angrily.

"You!" I yelled and stomped up the stairs.

"Wait a minute, I'm not done!" he yelled stomping up behind me. I ignored him and went into my room. I heard him running so I started to run. I got to my room and slammed the door. I pushed on it so he couldn't get in. He banged and started to push it open. "Lidia!" he yelled grunting as he tried to get in my room. I pushed my whole body on it so he couldn't get in. But he was pushing me back. I grinded my heels into the carpet but knew it was useless. He was stronger. He was laughing a little. Finally I failed and fell back as he burst open the door, causing it to hit my wall. He looked down at my angry eyes and smirked. I stood up and glared.

"I just want Grant back, okay?!" I said. His eyes became something different that I had only seen once but then it vanished.

"And I just want Kendra back!" he said.

"Fine!"

"Fine!" We both said to each other. We stared at each other for a moment then something quickly passed. We both reached for each other and we started to kiss. It was rough and forced. I grabbed at his hair and he grabbed at my waist tightly. I pushed him up against the wall almost knocking over a picture frame. Jack put his hands under my shirt as I rubbed myself against him. He groaned and flipped me over so he was pushing me against the wall. His lips were heating me everywhere. Everything was getting dizzy. Our tongues came together and I felt like I was floating. I sucked on his bottom lip and pulled back.

"I hate you!" I said gritting my teeth together.

"I hate you, too!" he said and picked me up. I kissed him again and down across his cheek and onto his neck. He dropped me down onto the bed and at that point my body was on fire. I put my hands under his shirt and started to lift it. His hands were on my stomach almost getting my shirt off. He grunted as I reached his chest. I frowned but kept kissing him. As I lifted off his shirt I saw the bruise. I paused and pulled back. I put my hand on his shoulder where the bruise was. He frowned then looked down. He jumped off me like I was a disease and pulled his shirt back on. "Jack," I breathed, my breath short. He clenched his teeth. "What was that? How did you get that?" He looked down, not meeting my gaze. I stood up, my body still hot. He wouldn't look at me. "Jack!" I demanded. He looked up. His eyes were mean and it scared me. I backed up a little.

"It doesn't matter," he said coldly.

"What is wrong with you?" I asked disgusted. He looked at me and I didn't recognize him.

"Why don't you do yourself a favor and stay out of my business!" My mouth dropped a little. I shook my head at him.

"Damn you," I said. He shook his head and without another word he left, slamming the front door. I stood there for a couple of minutes trying to replay the event over in my head. Why did he blow up like that? Something was going on. Damn! Why won't he tell me?! Ugh, I hate him! I guess we were done. I'm not talking to him. If he wants to be this way, then fine. He can, but I'm not taking it! Forget him!

Chapter 15

When my mom got home that night she came into my bedroom to see how I was.

"Lidia," she whispered. I looked up from my homework, my eyes sore and tired. She smiled. "You should be in bed." I smiled a little.

"So should you." She nodded her head and laughed.

"I'm just about to." I put my head back down on my books.

"Lidia is something wrong?" Mom came into the room and looked at me, worry in her eyes. She could always tell when something was wrong. I pulled off my reading glasses and set them on the night stand.

"Jack and I got into a fight."

"Aw, honey," she said and gave me a hug. I almost broke down, but I decided to stay strong. She pulled back and gave my shoulders a squeeze. "It's okay. Things like this happen in a relationship. It happens every day. You've just got to stick through and eventually things will work its way out." I smiled. But it's a fake relationship, Mom. Jack doesn't really like me and I...I'm still not sure. But he wouldn't want me, anyhow! And besides, we can't get along.

"Yeah, thanks, Mom."

She smiled and kissed my forehead.

"He'll come around," she whispered. I sighed. 'Sure, Mom. When pigs fly,' I thought to myself.

"You're probably right," I said, trying to reassure her. She smiled.

"Night, sweetie." She left my room, shutting my door. I looked out my window at the stars and smiled. I coughed loudly, which surprised me. Great. I was probably getting a cold.

"Ugh, Mommy!" I called with my nose getting stuffed up. My mom rushed into the room.

"Oh, what's wrong?" she asked. She put her hand to my head.

"I think you have the flu. I'll call the school."

I smiled.

"Thanks."

She nodded.

"Your father is coming home tomorrow." She said, shutting my curtains. Her voice was shaky, but brave.

"Why don't you go take a hot bath? I'll come and get you when your soup is ready," she said. I smiled. She left the room, but popped her head back in. "Oh and the meds are in the cupboard above the sink." I stood up and got my clothes together and then filled the big tub with all sorts of bubbles and soaps to make your nose open up and laid in it.

After I took my bath I forced a whole bunch of pills down my throat wanting to feel better again. Mom made chicken soup for me and I carried millions of blankets into the den and found a comfortable spot on the couch with a big bowl of hot soup. I turned on the TV to watch the Twilight Zone all day.

A call came later and I thought maybe it was dad, but mom came into the living room with a smile on her lips.

"It's Jack," she whispered. I narrowed my eyes at the phone held my hand out. "Here," she handed it over to me. I took the phone and turned it off. "Lidia!" she yelled. I rolled my eyes. "Mom, Jack was a jerk to me. I'm not giving in that easily." She sighed.

"OK fine, your decision." She went back to her office. He called 5 times that day. Every time I picked it up he tried to say he was sorry and not to hang up. The last time I almost talked to him but didn't. I lay down on the sofa and fell asleep.

The next morning I was feeling a lot better! Mom still made me stay home though. I sat on the sofa in my black and purple PJs with my hair in a messy bun. I was watching Tom and Jerry while eating a bowl of cereal as I usually do on Sunday mornings, when the phone rang in Mom's office. I didn't bother getting up.

"Mom, phone!" I yelled. I heard her answer it. I turned the TV up and sighed. My mom came out of her office a couple of minutes later trying to hide a smile. "What are you grinning at?" I asked frowning at her. She just pursed her lips together.

"Um. Can you go get the newspaper for me?" she asked. I put the TV on mute and stood up.

"Sure." I walked out the front door and saw the paper on the step.

"Good morning." I jumped and looked out at the driveway. Jack smiled, his white teeth gleaming in the sun, leaning against his car.

Chapter 16

"What are you doing here?" I yelled. He held a single red rose and put it to his nose to sniff it while still looking at me.

"I wanted to apologize for being a complete asshole to you." I shifted on the porch, my feet freezing. He came forward a little and held out the rose. "Please forgive me?" He put a little pout on his face that made me want to melt. I pushed a loose strand of hair behind my ear and crossed my arms realizing I was in my nighty, I looked away from him to show I was mad. He sighed. "Lidia," he said his voice soft, but amused. "Come on! Please?" I looked back at him and clenched my teeth. He was doing this on purpose. He hated me! Oh, but he was so cute! Get a hold of yourself, Lidia! "Pretty please." He pushed out his bottom lip and titled his head to the side like a lost puppy. I started to smile and looked away. "No! No, no! I saw that." I pursed my lips together trying hard not to laugh. He came up the steps and I kept looking away. "I saw that," he whispered. My stomach fluttered. He put his finger tips on my chin and drew my face over to his. His blue eyes glistened with excitement and something else. He put his lips right in front of mine. Teasing me. I stopped breathing for a moment and he just grinned. His bottom lip was rubbing against my lips and I shivered. "Please?" he asked again. His voice was low and seductive. I nodded staring into his eyes. He smiled and stepped back. I let out a breath I didn't know I had held. He got down on his knee and I stared at him. "Will you be my fake girlfriend?" he asked holding out the rose. "Again," he added. I laughed and smiled.

"Why not?" I said throwing my hands in the air. He grinned and stood up. I took the rose and smelled it.

"Mm, I forgive you."

He looked at me. Again the strange gleam in his eyes came as he looked at me. And not just at my body or face. He saw me. He

74

looked into me. I felt like I was losing myself into his eyes. His hand came up and touched my cheek with the back of it. A smile played on his lips. I just stared at him, feeling the warmth of his touch.

"Lidia!" We both jumped and turned to see my dad getting out of his car and coming up to us. I glared.

"Dad," I said through my teeth. He frowned at the two of us. Even Jack seemed to glare.

"Mr. Walker," Dad said to Jack.

"Sir," he answered. Dad looked at me.

"A little late to be wearing your bed clothes?"

I snorted.

"Dad I was sick." He made an 'O' with his mouth as he nodded. He went past me.

"Is your mother home?" he called.

"Yeah," I looked at Jack and he shook his head and rolled his eyes.

"Does your mom know?" he whispered.

I shook my head. "No, I didn't have the heart to tell her."

He nodded.

"Do you want to go to the playground?" he asked. I laughed a little.

"Sure," I looked down at myself and chuckled. "Let me get changed first." He laughed and we walked back into the house. I could hear my parents talking in my mom's office and urged myself not to listen. I laid the rose down on my dresser and changed quickly into a pair of jeans. As I unbuttoned my top I looked at the rose and smiled, biting my lip. My PJ top fell to the floor as I quickly grabbed a bra still looking at the rose. I picked it up and smelled it again.

"Oh I'm sorry!" I jumped slightly and turned around. Jack stood at the door as I clutched my bra to my bare chest.

"It's okay," I said softly. He stared at me. I turned my back to him feeling my face turn a little red as I slipped on my bra and found a T-shirt. I put down the rose and turned around to him and smiled a little. His eyes were glazed over and he still was looking at me.

"I-I didn't-I mean—"

"It's okay, chill." I laughed. "You already almost got my shirt off, so it's no different." He looked down and I swear I saw pink come to his cheeks. I grinned. "Is Jack Michael Walker really blushing?" I said putting my hands on my hips. His head sunk lower and I saw he was smiling too. "Aww, that's so cute." I walked over and looked at him. He lifted his eyes to me. His cheeks were red but he was smiling. I laughed. "Wow, not so tough anymore are you tiger?" My words were soft. He snorted a little.

"I don't know what you're talking about."

I laughed and patted his shoulder.

"It's okay, I won't tell the football team," I went out past him grabbing my shoes from the door. "You little..." He trailed off as I started running and laughing. I ran out the door grabbing my heavy coat.

"Lidia!" he yelled. I ran behind the yard and across Mr. Roger's yard and then found my way to the park. Jack caught up and pushed me as I stopped at the gate.

"Ow!" I yelled laughing. He laughed. He pulled his jacket on the rest of the way feeling the chilly air. I opened the gate and walked in. The grass was getting brown and crunchy under my feet and leaves fell onto the slide and the swing. I ran over to the swing and jumped on. Jack laughed and zipped up his jacket.

"You're real funny, you know that?"

I grinned. He ran over and put his hands on either side of the swing his face inches from mine. My breath caught in my throat a moment.

"Oh, really?" I asked. He nodded, smiling lightly. The smile was something I had never seen before on his face. Only in his eyes but it never spread this far on his lips. It made me melt inside.

"Yeah," he nodded. "And here we go!" I squealed as he pushed me up then went under me as the swing came back down. I laughed. I kicked my feet so I went higher and then felt the thing start to move. I slowed a little, laughing hard.

"Whoa, there girl!" Jack said grabbing my swing and stopping me.

"This thing isn't meant for us," I said

He laughed and nodded.

"Yeah I think it's been here for a while."

I nodded and looked around.

"It's been here for as long as I can remember."

Jack sat in the swing beside me and kicked a little to swing slowly.

"We lived in a small town before. I always loved it. Summer evenings in the fields. My friend and I had a tree we would always climb. It was great," he said quietly, gazing out across the park. "But when my mom broke up with her boyfriend there, she said she couldn't stand to stay. So, we moved." I watched his eyes. They were dark blue now. He looked over at me and smiled sadly. The smile obviously didn't reach his eyes. I didn't know what to say. I bit at my lip then turned in my seat to look at him. I put my legs up on his lap and smiled. He rolled his eyes and grabbed my legs. I jumped slightly surprised. He turned his swing and put my legs through his swing on either side of him.

"Does your mom have a boyfriend now?" I asked. He stiffened and I watched.

"Yeah, she does," the words were forced from his mouth. I could tell.

"Is some---?"

"What movie are we going to watch tonight?" he said, his words sharp and trying to tell me to shut up. I frowned.

"Um, I'm not sure."

"Something good." I nodded. His hand was on my leg and my heart was pounding in my chest. Good god, Lidia! His hand is just touching your ankle! Stop freaking out!

"Princess?" And there went the romance. I looked up and he was raising an eyebrow.

"What?" I asked my breath a little ragged.

"You're really out of it, aren't you?"

I smiled. I pulled my legs back from his swing and stood up. "Come on," I said. He stood up.

"What are we doing?" he asked. I smiled.

"Going on the slide."

Chapter 17

We played around in the park for about two hours. It was nice. Laughing and joking around with Jack. The wind picked up and played with my hair as I stood behind the ladder of the slide. "Boo!" Jack said through the ladder. I jumped slightly and hit his hand that came through the bars in front of my face. "Ow!" he cried and jumped back.

"Oh! I'm sorry!" I said almost laughing. He frowned at me and sucked on his index finger.

"That hurt," he said and came back to the ladder. He was on the outside and I was still on the inside.

"I said I was sorry," I said. He sniffed and looked down. I rolled my eyes. "What else do you want?" I said throwing my hands in the air. He looked up, his eyes a deep blue, making me stop and stare at him through the ladder.

"A kiss." My eyes got a little wide and I stared at him.

"Wh—"

"I think a kiss would help me forgive you."

I rolled my eyes. He leaned further in, his face inches from mine. The wind blew at the back of his head sending me a whiff of his hair.

"Fine," I said and stepped forward. I stood up a little. He stood very still as I reached in between the steps to his lips. I lightly kissed his lips. I opened my eyes a little watching him. His eyes were closed. I kissed him again, a shiver going up my spine. I wanted to do more than this! I closed my eyes and moved his lips with mine and finally he started to help. My body was on fire again. I wanted to press myself against him. To feel him….but the ladder was in the way. I trailed my tongue across his top lip and he seemed to groan. I smiled. I put my hand between the stairs and onto his jaw. He pulled back and looked at me. I frowned.

"OK…I forgive you." He was breathless. He had never done that to me before. I almost felt hurt. 'Come on! He doesn't want you,' I told myself.

"Um…yeah. I think we should head back and get ready for Candice and Tommy." He nodded and swallowed. He looked at me sucking on his bottom lip, his chest rising and falling.

"Yeah," he said in a low voice. I cleared my throat and went out from behind the slide steps and toward the gate. I turned around and Jack was still standing there, staring at where I had been. "Jack?" I asked. He looked up. His face blank. Then came toward me shoving his hands in his pockets. I walked out and Jack walked next to me as we went back to the house.

When we got back, Mom and Dad were in separate ends of the house. I walked into the kitchen and smiled at Mom. She just gave me a grim smile.

"Um, Candice and Tommy, some friends from school are coming over to watch movies. Is that alright?"

She smiled tiredly and nodded.

"Yes, of course baby. Do you want me to make you guys something?" she asked, looking at Jack behind me.

"No, that's alright. We'll take care of that. Why don't you go to bed?"

She sighed and then her eyes got big. "You can sleep in my room," I quickly said, understanding what she was thinking of. She smiled, relief showing in her face. She gave me a tight hug.

"Thank you, honey. I love you."

I kissed her cheek. "I love you too."

She pulled back and sighed once again.

"Well, I'm going to get a drink and go to bed," she said, matter-of-factly.

I laughed.

"Don't let the drink be too strong, okay?" She looked at me as if I'd just insulted her.

"Of course not!" she waved a hand at me then winked. "Maybe just two or three of your father's expensive Scotch."

I laughed and Jack laughed too.

"Go ahead," I said and patted her back as she grabbed a big glass cup and headed to the wine bar in dad's office. I laughed at her as she disappeared. I turned to Jack and he shook his head smiling. "Like I said, I like your mom." I rolled my eyes and slapped his shoulder.

"No chance in hell," I said. He snorted and laughed.

"We'll just have to see...but as for now..." He looked down at me with an amused look. "I have to be your boyfriend...but you know I don't think it's that bad." The words 'your boyfriend' rang in my head and made my stomach feel alive again.

"Wow, was that a compliment from Jack Walker?" I asked, putting my hand to my ear. He laughed and rolled his eyes. He pushed my hand down and I laughed.

"Yeah actually it was," he said smiling like the stars. He pulled me toward him and my breath caught again. "Lidia..." He trailed off and looked down. There was a slight pink hue coming to his cheeks. My heart was beating quickly now. Before he could say anymore, I inserted, "I think we should make the snacks now, before it gets too late." I pulled back and went over to the fridge. I closed my eyes just for a moment and then grabbed the milk and eggs. I turned around and saw Jack biting the inside of his jaw and looking at me. He then made a funny face.

"What are we going to make, boss?" he asked playfully.

I smirked. "Cookies. Want to help?"

He snorted. "I don't—."

"Here!" I gave him the milk jug and the eggs and he grabbed them before they fell. He looked at me under his eye lashes and I grinned. "You're so sweet. Now, let's go."

We made chocolate chip cookies. It was fun having Jack beside me mixing the batter, putting them on the sheets and putting them in the oven. I put the last tray of cookies in and shut the oven door. I sighed. Jack washed his hands while I grabbed a bit of left over cookie dough and ate it.

"Eww!" Jack cried looking at me in disgust.

"What?" I asked laughing. He scrunched his face up shaking his head. "Haven't you ever tried it before?"

"That's sick Lidia. There's raw eggs in there!" he said, pointing to the empty egg carton. I laughed.

"Try it!" I grabbed a spoon and put a little on it.

"No!" he said, laughing a little.

"Come on! It's good. Just try it!" I backed him up against the counter laughing. "Ugh! Just try!"

"No!" he yelled. I pushed his shoulder so he hit the counter and he saw he was pinned.

"Just try," I warned, smiling.

"I don't want to try it," he mumbled as I pushed the spoon to his lips.

"Yes, you do," I said laughing. "Jack! Just open your mouth!" I yelled. He huffed and opened his mouth. I put the spoon in his mouth and he chewed it up with his eyes closed.

"See? Now, how was that?" He opened his eyes and tasted it. He looked surprised.

"It's actually not bad." I rolled my eyes and threw the spoon in the dish pan.

"See! What'd I tell you?"

He laughed, put his hands on my waist and pulled my hips to him.

"I would do it again because I liked being backed up to the counter like this." He whispered low and seductively. A shiver coursed my body but I pulled back and gave a nervous laugh.

"You're so stubborn and perverted," I said rolling my eyes. He smiled at me. The doorbell rang and I jumped slightly.

"Come on," I told Jack as we made our way to the door.

Chapter 18

I opened up the door and Candice and Tommy stood there, smiling, but shivering from the cold. "Hey, guys. Come in," I said and let them in. I shut the door quickly, shivering myself. The air was getting cold.

"Ugh! I hate the winter!" Candice complained as she took off her layers of clothes. Tommy laughed and just took off his jacket.

"I have snacks and stuff but we still didn't pick out a movie." I said. Candice laughed.

"It's okay. We brought all three Back to the Futures and chips!" she pulled out a bag of chips. I smiled.

"Awesome. I love those movies."

Jack looked at me surprised.

"You like those movies?" he asked. I nodded.

"Yeah, my dad and I would have weekend movie nights and we would watch them." Jack was looking at me as if I was raised from the dead.

"Well," Candice said and took her seat on the sofa. "I'm ready to watch movies and drink something warm. What about you guys?"

Dad came out during the second Back to the Future movie and got into a discussion with Tommy and Jack about it. Candice and I laughed.

"It's cold in here. Let me start up the fire for you guys," he said and went over to the fireplace in the corner and brought the flames to life. Jack and I sat on the floor on a blanket with pillows propped behind our heads. We held hands and sat an inch apart but

Candice was completely curled up to Tommy beside me. She sighed and we all thanked my dad for making the fire.

"Night, Olli," Dad said kissing my head as he passed.

"Mm," was all I said. Jack gripped my hand tighter as he went past and I looked at him frowning. His jaw was stiff but then as my dad left the room he loosened up. "What's wrong with you?" I whispered. He looked at me and the fire danced in his blue eyes.

"Nothing," he said, with a shrug. I frowned. He was wearing a dark green long sleeved T-shirt which had ridden up a little on his side exposing a little black and blue mark. I looked at it and then up at him. He looked down as well and then covered it up quickly. He wouldn't look me in the eyes.

"Jack?" I whispered. He didn't respond. What was going on? Why did he have bruises everywhere? I didn't want to argue with him now. I sat back and laid my head on his shoulder. He flinched slightly but sighed and slouched more on the floor. I could smell his cologne and it smelled good. And I could smell the peppermint. I looked down at our hands and frowned. Why did I like the way our hands fit together? Why did I like the way he kept his hand over mine in a protective way? 'Remember Lidia, it's just for show. Don't forget that.' As if I hadn't already.

Candice and Tommy went home late that night saying that we should do it again sometime. Jack and I agreed. Jack left not long after. He seemed distracted and left quickly. I went to bed and sighed as I saw my mom in my bed. I pulled the half empty bottle of Scotch from her hands and covered her up with my comforter. I slipped on a pair of my shorts and a tank top, grabbed my pillow and a big blanket and went back downstairs to the sofa. I lay down and pulled the blanket over me while staring at the fire. It was peaceful. It felt like Christmas Eve when I would sneak downstairs after my parents had gone to bed and wait for Santa. The year I turned ten, I stayed up all night, waiting. That year I found out that Santa wasn't real.

Chapter 19

On Saturday morning, I stood up and pulled down the curtains in the living room at 8:30 a.m., knowing that I wasn't going to get up for about 5 hours and crawled back on the sofa. I stuffed my face into my pillows and sighed. My eyes drifted shut and I started to dream.

I was in a big open field. Birds sang and bees buzzed around me. I smiled. I was wearing a white summer dress with no shoes. But shoes weren't really necessary as I was standing on lush grass. It was soft; like sheep's fur. I smiled and closed my eyes. The air smelled like freshly cut grass.

"Lidia," a voice called. I opened my eyes and looked across the field and there was a big tree. It sprouted from the ground with big roots and the thick branches escaping from the top. I frowned slightly. Did I dream that? Then I saw someone on the tree. He jumped down and smiled at me. I recognized those blue eyes. I walked toward the tree and suddenly I was under its shade. Jack stood leaning on it with one of those heart melting smiles. "Lidia," he said, the word clear and full of passion. My heart was pounding in my chest.

"Jack, what are you doing here?" I asked. He walked forward with his lips looking amused.

"Me? You put me in here. You're dreaming of me," he said. My mouth fell open a little.

"Wh-what?" He smiled and I said, "I never dreamt about anyone but Grant in here, on this field! I don't dream about you!"

He smirked.

"I'm not Grant am I?" he asked, putting his hands up a little. I looked at him. He was wearing brown leather pants and a loose white shirt showing some of his chest. I tried not to seem distracted.

"Come with me, Lidia," he whispered, taking my hand.

"What?" I asked again. He took both of my hands and pulled me toward the tree. "What is this tree?" I asked gazing up trying not to look at our hands together.

"It's my tree. The one I had back home." I frowned at him and he smiled. "It's fun. I'll help you." I nodded looking into those baby blues. He climbed up on a branch and then helped me up. He held my waist as he looked at me.

"Jack," I said quietly. "Jack, I think I'm---"

****

I jolted upright on the sofa, my face sweating and my shirt sticking to my skin. I let out a breath and noticed that the sunlight was streaming into the big den. I groaned. I looked at my clock. 9:30 a.m. I only got one additional hour of sleep? Ugh! I stood up and my feet felt a little wobbly. I pushed back my hair and sighed. That was a very...that dream was amazing! It felt so real! But no! You were about to say something to him you would have regretted! Even if it was in a dream. You can't admit anything to yourself. I'd never had dreams about Jack before. That was the first time. I can't believe I dreamt that! I was so dizzy. I shuffled out of the den and walked to the kitchen where I heard the crunch of cereal as two people were eating and reading the newspaper. I walked over, my eyes a little foggy. My dad sat at one end with a cup of coffee and a bowl of cereal with his face stuck in a paper. Then, as I looked to the other, I looked down, then up. Old sneakers, faded jeans, tight white long sleeved shirt. I gulped. The newspaper covered his face. "What are you doing here?" I almost yelled. Both persons jumped and looked at me. Dad smiled.

"Morning Ollie," he said cheerily. Jack looked at me and grinned.

"Just waiting for you to get up." His eyes trailed their way from my bare legs to my shorts then my stomach, then up to my chest where I didn't have a bra on, then up to my eyes. "But I see you're a little...um...." He was a little pink in the cheeks and that's when I realized.

"Oh!" I said and crossed my arms over my chest, embarrassed. Dad just shrugged and started to read again. "I'm going to go get dressed." I said and ran to the stairs. I heard Jack laughing shyly. I smiled to myself as I went into my room hearing the snore of my mom still sleeping. I grabbed a pair of jeans, a blue shirt and undergarments and left, shutting the door. After a quick shower, I put on a little makeup and got dressed. I walked out and almost ran into my mom. She smiled at me in her messy hair.

"Hey, honey."

I smiled. "How'd you sleep?"

She grinned. "Great! Like a baby."

I laughed and kissed her cheek. She went into the bathroom as I went downstairs. Jack was still looking at the paper but not really reading it.

"Hey," I said quietly as I came downstairs. Jack looked up, his eyes surprised but sweet. "So, why are you here?" I asked as nicely as possible. He shook his head with a smile. Dad cleared his throat and looked at me.

"Oh, I didn't hear you," he said.

I rolled my eyes. "You never do."

He shrugged.

"You look nice," he said and I smiled a little at him.

"Thanks." I looked back at Jack.

"Um, do you want to hang out today?" he asked, a little unsure.

I frowned slightly.

"With Kendra and Grant?"

"No."

"With Candice and Tommy?"

He stood up, laughing a little.

"No. Just you and me." He paused and looked into my eyes. "Only if you want!" he said quickly. I smiled and bit at my lip.

"Sure." I said shrugging but seriously I was more tickled than anything. He smiled.

"Cool. I want to show you some really great places." I nodded.

"OK, hold on." I looked over at dad. "Dad, can I go?" He sniffed and pulled down the paper from his face.

"Yeah, go ahead," he said.

"Thanks!" I looked back at Jack. "One minute, let me go get my cell phone." He nodded and laughed as I ran up the stairs. Mom was coming out of the bathroom looking like crap. "Gosh, Mom," I said, surprised. She laughed.

"Sorry sweetie. Just a small hang-over." I laughed.

"OK well you can go back to sleep in my room if you like." She nodded.

"I might. Where are you going?" she asked. I ran into my room as she came in. I slipped on my shoes and grabbed my cell phone.

"Jack and I are going out. Call if you need me." She nodded and fell down onto my bed with a groan.

"Is your father still here?" she asked.

"Yep!"

She groaned again. I laughed, running down the stairs.

"Ready," I said, as Jack put on his jacket. He smiled.

"Great! Let's go, then."

Chapter 20

We got into his car and turned the heat up but it blew freezing air out.

"Sorry," Jack said as we drove.

"It's okay. I'm used to it." He nodded. He turned the music up a little. "You can change it if you want," he said casually. I smiled. I turned it to rock and left it low. I looked out the window as we passed the city. I frowned.

"Where are we going?" I asked. He smiled at me.

"It's a surprise." I gave him a questionable smile but nodded.

We came into a small town. The houses were a little shabby but everything looked small compared to the big city. "Where are we?" I asked. He looked out and in front of us was a little chapel then beside it was a small theater.

"This is Fairfield."

I looked around.

"Are we still in New York?" I asked. He laughed.

"Yeah we are. I used to live here." I looked over at him, stunned.

"How long did we drive for?" He looked at the clock.

"Two hours."

"Wow. I didn't realize," I said.

"I want to take you to the Diner." We pulled into a small diner that had an old sign outside saying "Lisa's Diner" that flickered every once in a while. The place looked like a trailer. It was silver and pink. Jack got out and stretched. I got out to look around. There were about 5 cars plus ours in the lot and people walked out even in the cold.

"This town is so small!" I said, surprised. Jack laughed and came over to me.

"It might be small but the hamburgers are the best!" We walked into the diner and people smiled and waved at us.

"Jack!" An older lady in her 30s behind the bar skated to us.

"Bonnie, hey," Jack said with a smile.

"Wow! You're looking so grown up! I hardly recognized you! But you look so much like your mother." She had bright red hair with red lipstick. She looked at me and grinned at Jack. "And who is this little girl?" she asked putting her hands on her hips. Jack blushed a little.

"This is Lidia...my girlfriend." Now I blushed.

"Well hello Lidia!" she put out her hand and I shook it.

"Nice to meet you," I said kindly. She sighed.

"I'm glad you're back to visit us. Now do you guys want something to eat?"

Jack nodded. "Of course. Does Bob have those hamburgers hot?"

Bonnie grinned.

"Well, yes, he does. You guys can go take a seat over there at the booth and I'll be over to get you something to eat." We nodded. Jack and I walked to the booth in the corner and sat down. Everything looked like it had come out of the 60s. It was amazing. I sat across from Jack and looked around.

"This is so cool!" I said, excited. He laughed quietly.

"Yeah, my mom and I would come here every week and get hamburgers and milk shakes." He looked down. "I miss it." I smiled at him.

"When was the last time you were here?" I asked.

"Um," he pondered. "It's been about a year..maybe a little longer. I don't remember." I nodded slowly. His hands were folded together on the table in front of us. He was looking down at them. I reached across and my fingers touched his hand softly. He looked up at me and I smiled a sweet and caring smile; the kind I would give Grant when he was sad. But somehow this was more important. He moved his hand and clasped it around mine softly. We looked at each other and I rubbed my thumb over his fingers. Jack's eyes were a blue that was so different and I liked it more then I should.

"Okay, so what can I get you dolls?" We both jumped and separated our hands. She didn't see. Jack cleared his throat.

"Um, two hamburgers and two chocolate shakes." My mouth dropped a little and I glared at him. "OK, coming up!" Bonnie left with a smile.

"Oh, honey, I just love it when you take control like that!" I said in an annoying Barbie voice. He smirked. "You know I can talk." He laughed.

"Yeah probably too much." I gasped. He laughed again.

"Seriously, though. Trust me when I tell you that this is the best stuff!"

I narrowed my eyes at him.

"Fine."

"This is good!" I sipped my milkshake, smiling. Jack laughed.

"Told you so." I shrugged and drank the rest of it. I sighed and sat back, holding my stomach. "Ugh I feel like I gained 20 pounds." Jack laughed and sat back too placing his hand on his stomach.

"Me, too." He burped and I laughed.

"How was it?" Bonnie asked picking up our empty cups and plates.

"Great!" I said. She smiled.

"Well great! I'm glad you both enjoyed it!" She skated back with our empty plates.

"I would trip and kill myself if I was her," I said watching her disappear behind the counter. Jack laughed.

"She's been working here for as long as I can remember. She's used to it." I smiled.

"So is this all you brought me here for?" I asked looking at him. He grinned.

"Nope. Come on." He stood up and we gave our money to Bonnie.

"You come back here again, Jack, and don't let it be so long." Jack smiled.

"OK, good seeing you, Bonnie." He waved as we headed out the door.

"Oh and you bring Ms. Lidia back too!" I laughed and Jack nodded. I kicked my feet at the dusty ground as I walked around to the car.

"So where next, Boss?" I asked. He laughed.

"Well, we'll have to see. I'm pretty sure we'll be okay but..." I raised an eyebrow at him.

"But what?" He shrugged and grinned.

Chapter 21

We drove on the outskirts of town on the small roads. I watched closely and saw that most of the leaves were off the trees. I shivered and Jack cranked up the heat. We slowed down as we came around a corner. On the right side of the road was a light green house with a long room on the left side. "There it is," he said. I looked curiously.

"What? It's a house. We could have seen that anywhere."

He rolled his eyes.

"It's not the house, it's that room on the end." I looked down and saw windows surrounding it. "So? It's a room."

He snorted.

"Just wait." He went back an alley down the road from the house and got out.

"What are we doing?" I asked. He smiled.

"Get out and I'll show you," I got out and covered myself from the cold wind. "This way," he said as we went through a field. "Dunk," he whispered as he crouched a little lower.

"What the hell are we doing?" I whispered in a yell. He laughed.

"You'll see." We made it across the lawn and over to the green house's yard. We hid behind a tree. Jack looked out at the lot but there were no cars there. He grinned. "Good. No one's home."

"What?" I asked. He grabbed my hand and we ran across behind the long side of the house. A small window was creaked open with a little pebble. Jack let my hand go and put his fingers up through the window and then opened it. "Jack!" I yelled.

"Shhh!" he yelled back.

"What are you doing?" I whispered. He grinned at me.

"We're going for a swim." My mouth fell and he laughed and opened up the window.

"But this is illegal! Sneaking into people's houses!" He laughed again and jumped in through the window. "Jack!" I yelled. I looked in and saw the nice deep dark blue pool. I raised an eyebrow. Jack stood at the bottom smiling like the fool he was. "Oh no!" I said shaking my head and stepping back. Jack laughed.

"Come on!"

I shook my head again. "We're trespassing!" I yelled.

He snorted. "I sort of know these people. I did this all the time! They won't even know."

"You're an idiot!"

He chuckled and it echoed through the room. There was a hot tub in the corner. I shivered.

"Lidia," Jack said drawing my attention. His blue eyes gleamed below me. "For once in your life, do something that surprises people." The words took me aback but they were kind. His lips had a little smile on them. I didn't know what to say. I had never done anything like this before. But does it matter? I mean come on! I think this would be fun. Plus, I was freezing.

"Fine!" I said and sat down then jumped to the ground. He laughed quietly and lowered me down. He stepped back and I felt the heat of the water breeze on me and smiled.

"So I hope you don't mind," he started as he pulled off his jacket. I raised an eyebrow. "But I didn't bring my trunks." He pulled off his long sleeved shirt exposing his nice chest. He smirked at me while kicking off his shoes then his socks.

"Wait, what?" I asked. He smiled as I stared at his chest.

"I'm getting in. I don't know about you." He went over to the edge and dove in, disappearing for a while and then coming back up. He shook his head and smiled. "Man, this is warm!"

"But I don't have a bathing suit! I can't get in!" I yelled frantically. He grinned.

"Well then I guess you can't get in, then, can you?"

I glared.

"I will get in." I took off my jacket then my shoes and socks. I hesitated for a moment.

"Oh what? The Princess is afraid?" Jack mocked, laughing. I turned to him and smiled devilishly.

"Actually, no." With that, I pulled off my shirt and threw it to the ground. His eyes got a little wide. I smirked and yanked off my belt. "How's the Princess now?" I asked, standing in front of him with my baggy jeans and bright red bra. His eyes were still wide but he smirked. I ran along the side of the pool then dove in the deeper area. The water felt so good on my cold skin. It made me tingle. I came back up, took a deep breath and laughed. Jack smiled at me from across the pool. "Wow! It feels so good!" I said and laughed. He did, too. I went back under and touched the bottom then saw Jack's leg and grabbed one. He yelled and I laughed as I came back up.

"I so scared you!"

He shook his head. "Did not!"

I laughed and held onto the edge. Jack looked at me and I smiled.

"Happy?" I asked. He frowned for a moment.

"Mm?"

"I did something I normally wouldn't do."

He nodded and smiled.

"Yeah." I dunked down and let the heat warm my body again. That hot tub in the corner looks really good right now.

"So where are the people that own this?"

He smirked.

"Some rich family bought this a couple years ago after the other man died. I would animal-sit for the man who used to live here and I would swim after taking his old dog out. After he died a couple years later his house went up for sale. But now the family barely comes around here anymore. Only in the summer. So I come every once in a while to swim." I shook my head.

"Only you." He grinned.

"And no one is ever out here, so they won't see us."

I nodded.

"It's cool," I said, looking around. "So do you take all your fake girlfriends out here?" I asked with a laugh. He looked at me, laughed and then swam over to me. He was two inches away from me and stopped, looking into my eyes.

"No, you're the first," he answered quietly. I swallowed, staring at him and then at his lips. I wanted to taste them again. The urge was fierce but I couldn't give in.

"Um," I thought. "Let's go get in the hot tub," I said and lifted myself out. My pants hung down and I laughed, as did Jack. I got out and water dripped all over me. My pants were heavy. I pulled them up a little. Jack jumped out and laughed.

"Nice red polka-dot underwear, Taylor." He said, laughing. I rolled my eyes and blushed a little. "Oh! Is Lidia Taylor really blushing?" he mocked. I laughed.

"Maybe!" I said. He grinned.

"Don't worry I won't tell the cheerleading team," he whispered.

"Brat!" I yelled laughingly. He giggled and I pushed him back into the pool. I laughed and ran to the hot tub. My feet slid a little as I ran but something quickly grabbed me.

"Jack!" I yelled. He laughed. He started backwards my feet slipping.

"Baby you're going in!" he said. I laughed then turned and grabbed onto him.

"Not without you!" He laughed as we slipped over the edge and fell in together. I let go of him as we hit the water and rushed to the top spitting out water and laughing. Jack came up laughing, too. We looked at each other and just kept laughing.

"Come on, Romeo! I'm freezing!" I climbed out again and Jack slapped my butt. I swatted at his hand laughing. I sat down on the edge of the tub and let my feet in. It burned!

"Is it hot?" Jack asked. There was a control on the side and he turned it on. Jets mixed the water up and I slowly slid my body into the water, wincing slightly.

"Oh man, it's hot!" I said and giggled. He laughed and got in next to me. The water came up to my waist and I stood in the middle.

"Wow!" Jack said his bare chest heaving up and down. It was so nice! Not the water. His chest. It was a little tanned with tiny freckles on it. I looked down at myself and saw I really was just in my red bra and pants. I felt suddenly self-conscious about my body. I wasn't the skinniest, but I wasn't the biggest. "Ooh!" he said, wincing. I laughed. He looked at me and we both froze. I felt like he was looking into me, feeling that I was a little uncomfortable. He sat down on the seat and I did the same slowly. It was silent for a while.

"Why do you like Grant?" Jack asked suddenly. I frowned.

"Um," I thought for a moment. "I'm not sure." I admitted. "I guess it's because he's…." Why couldn't I think of anything? This is nuts! I thought I loved Grant. But to tell you the truth he had no personality. For some reason he agreed with everyone and didn't stand for what he believed in. Jack waited. "I don't know. For once I'm not sure." Jack nodded slowly looking away. It was quiet. Then Jack looked at me, stood up then came to stand in front of me, grinning.

"Well, you're probably glad you got a fake boyfriend like me!" he said pointing to himself. I rolled my eyes. He crouched down and grabbed my legs. I jumped and stared at him. He smiled. His hands rolled down my legs to my knees and grabbed me there. He picked me up and I reached for his neck. He sat back down and put my legs on either side of him. I gasped, a little surprised. He was still grinning. I didn't want my hands on his bare shoulders but I didn't know where to put them. He had his hands on my back, comfortably. He looked at me and I could feel his chest on my stomach but I didn't want to think about it. The water made bubbles around us with a humming sound. "Lidia," he said calmly. "Look at me." I didn't want to, but I did. Before we both even knew it, we were kissing. It was eager and passionate. We were holding each other tightly, my hands on his neck and his somewhere on my back. I couldn't tell my head was dizzy. I only knew where his lips were and how they felt on me. He kissed down my neck and I gasped with the pleasure.

"Just for benefits?" I asked, my breath heavy. He nodded and came back up to my lips.

"No strings," he whispered. I nodded too, and forced his lips back onto mine.

"No strings," I repeated. I kissed down his jaw feeling a little stubble and his hands tightened on my back. I sucked on his neck then kissed up by his ear. He moaned a little. I came back to his mouth and crashed mine with his once again. It almost pained me because I was kissing him so hard. I felt it in my lower stomach. It hurt but it felt so good. I put my hands down onto his chest feeling him. His hands roamed my back and his fingers drifted under my bra. He was about to undo it. I didn't know what my mind was telling me.

The only thing I heard was. 'Just do it. You know you like him more than a friend or fake boyfriend. Do what you want.' That's what it was telling me. And that's all I wanted to do. No objections. Just go with it...just go--ACDC's "Back in Black!" rang from across the room. We both jumped and looked over. It was Jack's cell phone. It went off but I just looked at Jack and kissed his neck again.

"Ignore it," I whispered. He nodded and then his hand came down to my jeans. He went under them. I was so hot and it wasn't from the water! His hand accidentally went over the front part of my pants and I moaned in his mouth. This made him groan as I gripped his back with my hands as tight as I could. "Back in black!" rang again. I rolled my eyes and pulled back. Jack sighed and pulled his hands away from me looking over at his glowing phone on the floor.

"It might be important," he said, still out of breath. I nodded and he lifted me off him. I sat back down in the water and tried to get my head straight on again. What were you just doing with him? His hands were...very close to me. I wish maybe we could have---."Mom?" Jack answered kicking me out of my thoughts. Which was a very, very good thing! "Yeah, yeah I'm fine...Mom, I can't!...where are you?" There was a pause. He rolled his eyes. His pants drooped in the front and I forced my eyes to the window. "Right now? I'm busy...yeah, I know...OK fine. Yes, I will pick it up. Okay. Be there in a while...love you, too," he whispered quietly. I smiled and got out, knowing we were done. Which was probably a good thing. I didn't trust myself with him anymore. He looked back at me and his face was sad. "My mom wants me to pick something up and take it home." I nodded.

"OK, that's fine."

He smiled slightly.

"Want to come along?"

I smiled.

"Sure," I grabbed my shirt and sighed as the rest of my body was wet and soaking wet that is. So was Jack. I looked at him and he went to the other side of the room and came back with two big white towels.

"I think we'll have to stop at your house for you to change quickly," he said. I laughed.

"Yeah I think so." He gave me a towel.

"We'll put this under us when we get into the car." I nodded and yanked on my shirt and pulled my jacket around me. "It's going to be cold." he warned as we headed back to the window. I nodded.

"Yeah, I know," I said, already feeling the cold air. We got out easily and ran across the field shivering, but laughing. He put his arm around me and I could feel the warmth from his body next to mine. I laughed as our teeth chattered. We ran to the car and got in. It was still a little warm. "Ugh, I'm freezing!" I said and rubbed my wet hands together. Jack chattered his teeth and I laughed. We started up and drove out turning the heat up so our skin tingled and burned. "Thanks, Jack," I said with a smile. He glanced over at me and shrugged.

"Yeah, sure," he answered with a small smile. I turned the radio up and listened to some music.

Chapter 22

We got back to my house about 2 hours later. I dreaded getting out of the car and into the cold air. "We'll make a run for it," Jack said, reading my thoughts. I nodded. I jumped out of the car when Jack did, laughing as we ran to the door. I pushed open the door but it was locked. I laughed. "Lidia!" Jack yelled. I pulled my keys out of my bag but with my hands shaking they fell out and Jack laughed and chattered his teeth. "Just go!" he yelled. I laughed and pushed the key into the key hole and threw open the door. We stumbled in laughing. He slammed the door shut with his foot. I pulled off my jacket and threw it on the floor.

"It's warm!" I yelled with pleasure. Jack laughed. "I'm going to go get changed. Do you need jeans?" I asked as I started for the stairs. Jack nodded.

"Um, yeah if you can find any." I nodded.

"You can borrow some of my dad's."

I got changed quickly and Jack came in wearing a pair of my dad's old jeans. They fit him pretty well. I smiled.

"Not bad, Mr. Walker," I said and he rolled his eyes. I combed out my wet hair and was about to put on some makeup when a hand caught my wrist. I looked at Jack, frowning.

"What's wrong?" I asked. His hand was gentle on my wrist.

"Don't put any on." I was watching his eyes. But they were just kind.

"Okay," I said and put down my eye liner pen. I smiled.

"We have to go, anyhow," he said as he let go of my wrist and cleared his throat.

"OK then, let's go." We went back to the car and this time I dressed warmer. We headed down the road and into the city. "Where are we going, anyhow?"

"My mom's work. She works at a restaurant in the city."

I nodded.

"And why are we going there?" I asked. He sighed.

"She wants me to pick something up to take home. Probably something for a friend." I smiled. "Oh okay." We drove up to a small restaurant and got out. I wrapped my scarf around my neck tighter and we walked up to the door. Our hands accidentally touched and then they automatically entangled together. It didn't really feel like a surprise because we had always done it every time we walked into the school. We walked in and behind the counter was an older woman with dark blonde hair who was very short.

"Mom," Jack said and the woman looked up from a note pad. Her smile brightened and her blue eyes gleamed. Now I know where Jack gets those eyes from.

"Hey, honey," she said, coming out from behind the counter. She put her hands on her hips and beamed at him.

"Mom, um, this is Lidia," he said, pointing down to me. I smiled at her. Her eyes went to our hands then up to me and gave me a heartwarming smile.

"So, you're Lidia? Jack has told me a lot about you. But he never introduced me to you!" She gave him a mean look and then smiled at me. I laughed.

"Mom," Jack mumbled, getting embarrassed.

"My name's Jane," she said sweetly. I smiled.

"It's nice to meet you."

"Yes, finally!" She gave Jack another look and I laughed. "So Lidia, what did my son here get you to do with him today?" I looked at him and he stared at his mother.

"Well he took me back where you guys lived. We went to Lisa's Diner to eat." His mom raised an eyebrow at Jack.

"You didn't, did you?" she asked, almost laughing.

"Excuse me?" I asked. Jack looked a little pink in his cheek. She looked at me.

"Did he take you to the pool?" My mouth almost fell a little but I laughed.

"Yeah actually he did. I had a lot of fun." Jane smiled at me and it had more of something admiring in it.

"Jack never takes girls there. You must be very important to him," she said quietly and then winked. I blushed. I was the first girl he took there? Wow. That's um...that's really sweet. But stop thinking about him like that!

An hour later and Jane and I were still talking. She was so nice. Jack lounged beside me looking like he was about to fall asleep.

"Oh it was so funny! When Jack turned 10 he was still wetting the bed—."

"Okay, that's enough!" Jack said looking like he was about to jump out of his seat. I laughed.

"Oh, no, I want to hear this!" I said and Jane laughed.

"No, no, no I think it's time we go now. Mom where's the stuff to take home please?" Jane pouted, but smiled.

"Okay, fine. But on one condition." Jack narrowed his eyes playfully at her.

"And that would be?" he asked. I smiled. She leaned over the table looking him straight in the eyes.

"You have to bring this adorable and amazing girl of yours to dinner next weekend." He clucked his tongue and looked at me.

"What do you say?" he asked. I smiled and nodded. He looked back at his mom. "It's a deal. And you never bring up that conversation again."

"Well I don't know—." she started but he growled and she laughed. He creaked a smile. "Okay, okay, I will try not to say that you peed your pants during your play at school." His mouth fell open and Jane and I burst out laughing.

"You little brat," he said shaking his head, his cheeks a little red.

"Awe, look he's blushing again!" I said, pointing to his cheeks. He grabbed my hand and chomped his teeth down close to it. I giggled and pulled it back.

"You both are ganging up on me. It's not fair," he muttered. Jane laughed and left the room for a moment. He spun on the stool and looked at me.

"What?" I asked innocently. He shook his head and I laughed.

"Okay, here we go." She brought out a bag with a bowl of soup and homemade bread. "Take this home and put it in the fridge right away. I don't want it to spoil." I saw a bruise on her arm as she gave the bag to me. I frowned. "Now you two have a good day and don't get her into too much trouble," she said pointing a finger at Jack. He smirked.

"I won't but she might get me into trouble."

I gasped.

"Will not!"

He grinned.

"OK, honey. Well, I'll see you next weekend, Lidia," she said and gave me a small hug.

"Thanks, Jane."

She smiled.

"Oh and Scott will be there, too." Jack almost lost his balance and looked at his mom. I stared at him, surprised. He was tense.

"What?" he asked his mom. She gave a nervous smile and nodded.

"He might come. I'm sure he'd be happy to meet—."

"No," he said suddenly, strong willed. I looked at him, surprised.

"Oh, come on, Jack!" I complained.

"No way in hell is she meeting him," he said through gritted teeth, ignoring me. I was staring at him. What was going on?

"Jack, come on. It'll be fun," I said. He looked at me and his eyes were mean and something like hatred filled them. I flinched.

"We're leaving," he said and turned.

"Jack," Jane called making him stop. His shoulders were so tight and his jaw was set. His eyes were blazing. He turned. Her eyes were teary. "Come here," she whispered. He clenched his hands but walked over to her. "Give me a kiss." He gently reached down and gave her a small peck on the cheek. She whispered something to him and I watched, my eyes a little wide. He nodded but his eyes didn't change.

"Mom," I heard him whisper, his voice pleading. I had never heard him sound like that before. They were whispering. "Fine." he finally said. "But if anything…," he whispered the rest.

"OK well you're coming over this weekend. Don't worry about it! I'll make something very good. OK?" she asked me.

"Yeah OK." I smiled. I was still so confused but nodded. Jack wouldn't meet my gaze.

"Bye," Jack mumbled and started to leave.

"Have fun!" his mom called, her voice a little shaky.

"Bye," I called back, feeling a little confused. Jack stormed off ahead of me and I followed almost at a run. "Jack! Jack!" I yelled. He put the food in the back seat and stood there for a moment then turned to me. "What the hell was that about?" I asked my voice making puffs of smoke from the cold air. He was biting the inside of his mouth hard trying not to yell.

"It's nothing. Let's go." I frowned.

"Jack…," I said, stopping him as he went around the car. He looked down. "What's wrong?" I asked. He looked up.

"Why won't you listen to me?"

The words caught me off guard.

"What?" I asked surprised. He looked away, his jaw clenching. I heard him mumbling but I couldn't hear. "What are you talking about?"

He shook his head.

"Never mind," he said and moved around me, his head still low. He got in and it took me a moment to regain myself before getting into the car.

Chapter 23

We started out towards the bad part of town and I began to get worried. Jack didn't talk very much. I didn't know what to say. Remember we're just faking this whole thing; he doesn't have to like you. Which he doesn't. He probably doesn't even like being my friend. I looked out the window and realized that this was nowhere close to where I lived. This was a whole other country! This was the poor side of town. I lived in the fancy part. I looked at Jack and he seemed completely at ease.

"Jack," I asked. He looked over at me for a moment and then back at the road.

"What?" he asked flatly.

"Where are we going?" He snorted.

"My home." I gulped a little. My parents told me I could never come on these roads. They were dangerous but if Jack knew what he was doing then I should trust him. We pulled up alongside the curb and I looked up to see a run-down building. Trash was strewn across the walk and loud booming music echoed through the streets. Jack got out and got the stuff. I slowly got out and looked up again at the apartment building. "This is it," Jack said looking where I was. "Home sweet home," he muttered and started for the entrance. This is the exact opposite of where I thought Jack lived. I thought he lived where Kendra or Grant and I did. Some place nicer. "Hurry up," Jack said and I ran across the walk beside him. We went up and Jack pulled out a whole bunch of keys then we went in. I followed him as we took the stairs and went up three floors. I could hear shouts from other doors and banging and music. It scared me a little. We got to a room and he unlocked several locks. Then opened the door. "Go ahead," he said and motioned me forward. I went in quickly. He came in and relocked all the locks. I turned and looked at the apartment. It was a whole lot smaller than my house but it had a cute kitchen and a small living room then a hallway going back somewhere. Probably the bedrooms. Jack came in and sat the bags on the counter then put everything in the fridge. "Not what you expected, was it?" he asked in an amused angry/sad sort of way. I turned to him but he was loading stuff in the fridge.

"Not exactly," I said quietly. He snorted.

"Did you think I lived where you did?" he asked. I shrugged and looked down. I did. I had never been here before.

"Has Kendra been here before?" I asked.

He stopped what he was doing and turned around to me. "No," he said. I frowned. Why hadn't she? They had been dating for what, a year? And he never brought her here. He finished and got a drink of water.

"Why bring me here?" I asked. He looked at me and put down his cup slowly. He looked down for a moment and then up, his eyes confused.

"I'm not sure," he answered. It was silent for a while. "I think I'm going to go change my pants," he said, looking down at my dad's jeans. I nodded. "You can come with me if you want," he said and we went down the hallway and to the first door on the left. It was a tiny room. There was a small single bed stuffed in the corner with a dresser at the end and a desk right across from it. The rest of the room was piled with clothes. He went over to the dresser and yanked the draws open. I looked around at the band posters and gray sheets messed up on his bed. It smelled like him. I walked over to his bed and sat down. It was lumpy and my butt went deep into it.

"So, this is your room," I said as he went across the room and picked up a pair of jeans and sniffed them.

"Yeah," he said and sniffed them again. He shrugged.

"It's nice."

He snorted and shook his head. "I'm sure!"

110

"No, really," I said. He turned and looked at me. "It's not like my house but sometimes I wish this is where I lived. Some place where it felt like home. My house is just an empty hollow cave. This," I said pointing around to the room, "is cozy and feels like a home." He looked me in the eyes and I gave a small sad smile.

"Mm," he answered and turned around. He unzipped his pants and I gasped.

"What are you doing?" I asked turning around. He laughed.

"Changing! What does it look like?" I glanced over at him as he pulled off my dad's jeans; he had red boxers on. I raised an eyebrow as I looked at his legs then up his body. He pulled up his jeans then turned to me and zipped them up and winked. I rolled my eyes. "Nothing you haven't seen before," he said. I blushed a little and looked down.

"Oh look, she's blushing again," Jack said coming over to me. I looked up as he bent over a little and wiggled his eye brows. "Decided yet that you're madly in love with me?" I shook my head.

"Not even close," I said getting closer to him.

"Really?" he asked. I nodded. His shirt had come up from pulling his jeans on and was lifted to see his left hip. There was a bruise. I frowned. I reached up and put my fingers on it. Jack flinched slightly and stood back. I stood up and followed him as he walked backwards trying to get out of my reach. His back hit the wall. I kept my fingers on it. Then I lifted up the shirt a little so that my eyes could focus on the bruise. It was the size of a baseball. I looked up on the verge of tears.

"Jack…," I whispered. His eyes were hurt but he was trying to cover it up. He reached down and took my hand and pulled his shirt back down over it. He brought my hand up to his lips and kissed it. I was shocked at this but just looked at him.

"Don't worry about it," he said and shrugged. "We should probably get you home soon, Princess," he said with a geeky smile as he pushed around me to grab his wallet from his jeans. I stared at the wall. Why was he hiding something from me?

"What time do your parents want you home?" he asked. I turned around.

"Um, er, I'm not sure." He laughed a little and nodded.

"OK, well let's get something to eat because I'm starving!" he said, patting his stomach.

"When aren't you?!" I said and laughed. He shrugged and grinned.

We got something to eat at his house and then headed back to mine. I got out of the car and he did, too. "Listen I should probably just go back home. My mom is going to be getting off work soon." I nodded.

"Yeah, I probably will have to deal with the parents inside." I said rolling my eyes. He smiled.

"Good luck."

"Yeah I'm going to need it," I reached for the door but stopped and turned around. "Thanks, Jack. I had a lot of fun today. I think I needed it. It's just with everything that's going on..." I trailed off. I looked at him. Now is not the time to tell him. "Thanks," I said quickly. He nodded.

"See you on Monday." He leaned forward and kissed my cheek and quickly went to his car. I was stunned once again. After he left, I let out a girlie giggle and sighed. I opened up the door, feeling giddy.

"Mom, Dad, I'm home!" I called. They were in the den arguing but stopped when they saw me.

"Oh, hey, honey," Mom said, pushing her hair back with a smile. Dad nodded at me looking like he was sweating badly. "How was your day?" she asked sweetly. I bit at my lip.

"Um, it was good. Jack and I ate at a diner then went—." I stopped mid-sentence. If my parents found out about that, they would murder me. "Um, just hung out." Mom smiled and nodded. "I'm going to my room," I said and left quickly. I heard them muttering some words but I ignored it. I shut my door and stripped out of my clothes, getting into something comfortable and started to read with a smile on my face.

Chapter 24

I went out running on Sunday morning then came back, got a bowl of cereal and watched cartoons like I did when I was 8. It was fun. Monday came quickly and I found myself looking out the window at the storm that had covered everything in a thin layer of snow. I smiled. I ran downstairs upon hearing the knocking on the door. I swung open the door to find a shivering Jack. I laughed.

"Not too hot are you now, hot stuff?" I teased. He rolled his eyes with a smile and pushed past me and entered the house.

"Damn, I hate the cold!"

I laughed.

"If only you would wear more than that leather jacket."

He turned to me.

"It was my uncle's," he said softly. I frowned. "He died a couple of years back. Closest thing I had to a father." I was silent.

"Oh, I'm sorry," I said quietly. He shrugged.

"Just don't insult the jacket," he said and posed. I laughed and rolled my eyes.

"Come on, I think my mom made something to eat. Want anything?"

He grinned.

"Yes!" We went into the kitchen to find my dad sipping coffee and reading something and my mom drinking a glass of water by the bar.

"Hey Jack!" she said and smiled. "I just made some breakfast. Would you like any?" He nodded eagerly.

We ate breakfast with my mom and dad. It was a little strange, but I found that I was relaxed. They liked him. They actually liked him. Dad wasn't too fond of Grant but he seemed to like Jack. Surprisingly. Wait, why do you care if they like him? You're not really dating him, stupid! I suddenly lost my appetite and put down my fork and took a sip of water. Right, it's not real. He doesn't like you...a churning went through my stomach and I thought for a moment I might throw up but then regained myself.

"You okay, Lidia?" Jack asked from across the table. I looked up and he actually looked concerned. The churning started again. He was faking it. He was faking everything. 'He doesn't like you!' I was yelling at myself. I felt like I was going to...no...oh no!

"Lidia!" someone yelled. I pushed back my chair and ran upstairs holding my hand to my mouth. I ran into the bathroom and slammed the door shut and puked into the toilet.

If I thought eggs would look like that, I would have never eaten eggs in my life. Jack pushed open the door as I was wiping the back of my hand over my mouth. His eyes were wide.

"Lidia, are you okay?" he asked as he ran over and sat down beside me. I nodded.

"I'm fine," my throat felt raw. He put his hand on my shoulder and massaged it. I closed my eyes and suddenly realized why I had barfed. I opened my eyes.

"Maybe—."

"No!" I pushed his hand off me and scooted away. His eyes looked hurt. I looked at him. It was his fault you're barfing your not so good looking eggs. "I said I was fine!" I said my voice louder. I grabbed a towel from the towel rack above my head and wiped my mouth again, still tasting the eggs.

"I was just going to say why don't you go lie down." I shook my head and grabbed the wall and started to stand. I started to slip and Jack was right there holding on to me. I pushed him back and growled.

"I can do it myself!" I yelled. He frowned. I stood up and leaned against the wall trying to settle the dizzy feeling. I went to the sink and washed out my mouth then brushed my teeth. Jack watched me. "Don't you have anything else to do?" I snapped as I finished. He clenched his teeth together.

"Lidia!" Mom said, as she and dad came up the stairs. "Oh, honey! Are you okay?" she asked as she came in past Jack. I nodded as she put her hands on my face. "You look pale sweetie. Let's go let you lie down a bit. I'll call the school."

"No!" I said, making everyone jump from my outburst. Dad frowned and Mom just looked worried. "Honey—"

"Mom, it's okay. I'm fine. I think it was just the eggs." I wouldn't meet Jack's eyes. I couldn't. I was lying of course but I didn't want him to know.

"Alright, if you think you're okay."

I nodded.

"I am." She pulled me out of the bathroom and we went downstairs. "I think we better just leave," I told Jack who I knew was behind me, watching me. He didn't answer. I put my jacket back on, my hands trembling a little. I grabbed my backpack and Jack followed behind me as we went out.

"Bye!" Mom called. I stopped on the porch and looked at Jack's crappy car.

"I don't have 4 wheel drive," he mumbled. I nodded.

"We'll take mine," I said quietly and I headed to my black jeep. I got in and started it up shaking a little. Jack got in the other side. The jeep didn't have very good heating so we were frozen until a block from the school when the heat finally kicked in. I put my gloved hands in front of it trying to steal the warmth. Jack just looked out the window. We didn't talk as we headed into the school. He took my hand but it felt weird with our gloves on. We smiled at people, putting on like we always did when we got mad at each other. But this was deeper. This was different. He walked me to my locker, we let go our hands.

"I'm going to class," he muttered. I nodded as I grabbed my books out of my locker and he disappeared in the crowd. I stared after him. I should go talk to him. Make up for being a jerk. 'No, no, Lidia. Don't. You're going to be breaking up soon enough anyhow. It isn't working with Grant or Kendra. Why bother going on anymore? They don't want us back.' But something inside of me wanted them to not love us. That I agreed to do this fake relationship for a reason. I didn't know what the reason was though. I frowned as I walked to class and sat in the back.

"Lidia," a sweet voice said. I looked up and saw Grant.

"Hey," I said and looked down picking at my finger nail.

"So, how was your weekend?" he asked causally. I shrugged.

"Pretty good. Yours?"

He shrugged, too. "So, so."

I nodded, still looking down.

"I wanted to talk to you, Lidia—."

"OK, class. Get settled in. We're about to start." I looked up and saw Grant rolling his eyes.

"I'll find you later today," he said and I nodded. The sound of his voice wasn't like Jack's. It didn't affect me like Jack's did. I didn't know why. Why did Jack's voice affect me so? I never liked him. Or did I? I shook my head and listened to our teacher.

Chapter 25

Next thing I knew it was Thursday. Nothing really happened. Jack didn't come over to the house after school, we both didn't talk. But it wasn't me. It was him. Something was wrong. He seemed really distant. We were going to have dinner with his mom on Saturday. 'Wow that's going to be a trip in the park!' I thought sarcastically. We didn't even hold hands that much anymore. I haven't even talked to Kendra or Grant. I was too swamped with schoolwork. Algebra was kicking my ass. It snowed more and it was two weeks until Christmas. School would be ending for the holidays in about a week. Jack and I walked out of school quiet as usual. We got into the jeep and I started it up kicking my foot trying to get the snow off. I sniffed and wrapped my scarf tighter around my neck.

"My mom said, um, that I should pick you up and bring you to the house since the streets aren't safe." I looked over at him, surprised at his voice. It was throaty and sounded sick but it was the first I'd heard all day. He looked at his hands.

"OK, what time?" I said and drove out the school gate. He shrugged and sniffed.

"6:00 p.m.?" I nodded. We drove to my house where Jack's car sat covered in a thin layer of soft puffy snow. I turned off the car and turned toward Jack.

"Jack, listen. I'm sorry about Monday…it's just that I wasn't feeling like—."

"It's fine," he said and looked over at me. Something stirred in his eyes and he let a small smile spread to his lips. "I've been….a little sick this week…is all." He said quietly. I looked at him and searched for anything. Why was he acting this way?

"I'm worried about you," I whispered almost too low for anyone to hear. Jack half smiled at me.

"Don't worry about me, Taylor." I looked down at my gloved hands.

"I'm sorry if I did anything to make you mad." I said. He laughed.

"Isn't that what we do? Get each other pissed off?" He lifted my chin with his finger and smiled at me. "I think it's kind of sexy when you're mad." I rolled my eyes and laughed.

"Sure," I said. He dropped his hand from my chin and sighed.

"I'm not sure Grant and Kendra want us back, Princess," he said quietly looking down then looked up through his eye lashes. I bit at my lip and nodded. "When do you want to break up?" he asked, trying to cover the sadness in his voice. It still leaked through. The thought of breaking up, the thought of actually not having Jack take me to school or hold my hand as we walk into school. The thought of not being able to touch Jack or to fight with him made my heart heave. I couldn't live without his soft rough hands. But why? Why did my heart want this? Why did my body yearn for him? My lungs had almost stopped too, thinking about it. I looked at him and swallowed.

"I don't know," I said. He nodded.

"Well after this weekend, I guess," he said and shrugged. He winced. I stared at him, my eyes a little wide. "Gym practice," he stated quickly. Too quickly. I nodded, not believing him.

"Um, do you want to come in?" I asked hesitantly. He bit the inside of his jaw thinking. Then frowned.

"I can't...I have to be home when my mom gets home...it's just that she isn't...never mind."

I frowned.

"Is there something wrong with your mom?" I asked, concerned. He shook his head.

"No...she's OK."

I nodded slowly.

"I'll call you later or something," he said and got out. I did the same, slinging my backpack over my shoulder.

"Bye," I said as he got into his car and drove off. 'I'm so damn sick of this!' I thought to myself as I slammed the front door shut throwing off my shoes. What the hell is going on with him? I know we just made up and stuff but there is something that he isn't telling me! I want to know the truth. Tomorrow I am going to force it out of him. Mom came in, looking worried.

"Lidia, are you OK?" she asked. I nodded.

"Yeah I'm fine." Dad came in behind her and smiled at me. I frowned at the two of them. They looked relaxed for some reason. "What the hell are you guys grinning at?" I muttered.

"Watch your tongue," Dad warned. I put my hands up in surrender. Mom sighed.

"Your father and I decided we want our marriage to get better, so we're going on a marriage retreat on Monday and then coming back next Monday." I raised an eyebrow.

"Well...good," I said, not sure. Mom nodded.

"So, will you be okay by yourself?" she asked. I bit my lip so hard I tasted blood in my mouth. "Yeah, it's fine. You guys leave me alone all the time," I said, coldness seeping into my words. They didn't notice.

"Okay, good. We'll have enough food and I'll leave some money so you can order pizza and stuff." I looked away and crossed my arms. "Something wrong, sweetie?" she asked. I grabbed my backpack and avoided their eyes.

"No. I'm going to do my homework." I went up the stairs, passing their stupid faces. I went up into my room and dropped my bag to the ground realizing I had no homework today. I got out one of the books I hadn't finished, slipped on my reading glasses and started reading. Trying to transition from one world to another.

It was 6:00 p.m. when my mom called me down for supper. I told her I wasn't hungry. I didn't feel like eating. I didn't want to go downstairs. I looked out the window at the dark sky and saw that it was clearing a little. But this close to the city, you couldn't see the stars. I sighed and got back to my book. My phone vibrated on my nightstand but I didn't feel like looking. It vibrated again and I groaned and picked it up.

"Yes?" I asked.

"Lidia!" Jack said, relief in his voice. I was worried.

"Hey, what's wrong?" I asked. He sighed.

"I got into a fight with my mom and her...boyfriend. I'm out driving around and I can't go home. Could I maybe stay with you tonight?" I was stunned. "I mean, I can go someplace—," he said after I didn't answer.

"No! No, no. You can come over! I was just thinking. Yeah, my parents are home so you'll have to sneak in through my window but they're leaving early tomorrow morning for work. So, yeah. Come over," I said quickly.

"OK, which window is yours?" he asked. I looked out the window and saw the road.

"It's two windows from the front door. The porch is a wrap around so you can jump up there. There's a stool by the side where I used to...," I trailed off. He snorted.

"You've sneaked out before?"

I was quiet.

"No comment."

He laughed. It rang like bells and I smiled. He was okay.

"I'll park my car down the street. Have your window open and turn the heat up. I'm freezing my ass off."

I laughed.

"Okay." I hung up, jumped out of bed and started to pick up my clothes and piled them on my dresser and into my dresser draws. I went to the window and opened it only to realize that I was wearing shorts and an old T-shirt. I grabbed my school sweat shirt and pulled it over me. I went to my mirror and fixed what was left of my makeup and nodded to myself. Good enough. I heard the noisy car slow down near my house. Whatever he was hiding, I was going to force it out of him tonight. But just the thought of having Jack in my room, at night, sleeping made my head think crazy thoughts.

Chapter 26

I turned the dial up on the heaters and heat blazed from it. Jack came from Mr. Rogers' yard and saw me. He sighed as he looked up at the house. He climbed the porch with a brown backpack over his shoulders and looked in at me when he arrived at my window.

"Princess," he said and cracked a smile. I rolled my eyes. He came in, his snow boots bringing the puffy white snow into my room and on my toes.

"Aw man, Jack!" I whispered in a yell. I tip-toed to the window and shut it shaking. "Take off your boots." I said and he did. He put them in the corner then peeled off his jacket.

"Damn its cold," he muttered and put his hands over the heater dunk. I went over to my closet and grabbed the old mattress that my friends would sleep on and pulled it out.

"Yeah, it's winter," I said sarcastically. He smirked. He helped put the mattress on the other side of my bed so if my parents came in, they wouldn't see him immediately. I brought out a pillow and a Barbie comforter and threw them on his bed. He looked up at me from under his bangs.

"You're kidding?"

I gave him a smug look. "Nope."

He sighed. Then I heard someone walking up the stairs.

"Lidia?" my mom called.

"Shoes!" I said and grabbed Jack's hand running toward my open closet door. He laughed and I turned and clamped a hand over his mouth. He winced. I frowned. The steps got closer. I pulled my hand away from his mouth and saw it. The cut on his lip. My mouth hung a little then I looked up into those blue eyes and glared.

"Lidia…I think we should talk…" Mom said, knocking on my door. Jack's eyes were sad. I shoved him in the closet and shut the door just as my door peeked open. I smiled as mom entered the room. She smiled at me. "Something wrong, honey?" she asked. I shook my head and headed over to my bed where my book lay open. "Lidia, are you okay? You seem different somehow," Mom said, as she sat down on the bed. I gritted my teeth together. I sighed.

"Mom, I'm fine. I've just been busy with school and stuff." She frowned.

"Is everything okay with you and Jack? Are you on the pill honey? I don't want you getting pregnant." My eyes bulged from my eyes and I heard a faint laugh. I coughed.

"Oh my gosh, Mom," I said. "I'm not having sex!" I yelled. She shrugged.

"OK, honey," she said doubtfully.

"You know, Mom…," I trailed off and looked away.

"Please don't get mad at me. I'm only worried. Why don't we do something tomorrow after I get back from work? Since your father and I have been fighting, it's been hard for us to do anything. Besides me sleeping in your room." She smiled and laughed. I didn't.

"Yeah, fine," I said quickly. She sighed and patted my knee.

"Goodnight, honey. I'm going to bed early because of work and your father will, too." I nodded. She kissed my head and left the room. I put my hands to my head and sighed. After she left, I opened the closet door and found Jack looking at a picture of someone. He looked up at me and put the picture down on a pile of clothes. Heat rose in me at the sight of him.

"Your Mom—." I grabbed his shirt. He looked stunned.

"I want to know the truth," I whispered fiercely. He frowned. I dropped his shirt and picked it up. There was another bruise forming and the one on his hip yellowing. He looked away, teeth clenched.

"I don't—."

"If you don't give me an answer I swear to God...." I warned, my hands almost shaking. He looked at me with sad eyes.

"I think I should leave," he said and moved around me. I shook my head tasting blood in my mouth again. I grabbed him by the shoulder and turned him around.

"Jack," I breathed. "I want to know now." With that, I pulled him in and mashed my lips against his. He acted a little late but slowly put his arms around me pulling me tighter against him. But somehow it wasn't tight enough. I kissed him, putting every ounce of everything I felt about us. Finally I pulled back, both of us panting. His lip was bleeding a little bit but he didn't seem to notice. He was frowning with his blue eyes dull.

"Lidia," he said his voice sad and miserable. I shook my head. He looked away then nodded. "OK," he breathed. "I'll tell you," he whispered.

Chapter 27

I turned out the light and turned the one on at my night stand. Jack sat on my bed with his legs stretched out leaning on the post. I sat leaning on the head rest. Jack sighed and looked away from me.

"My mom met a guy at a bar a couple of months ago. Scott. When he first started coming over, he was nice and Mom loved him. I even thought he was cool. He started living with us about 2 weeks after they met." He bit the inside of his jaw trying to find the right words. "One night, he and my mom came back to the house and he was drunk. My mom was trying to get him into bed when he told her to get him another beer. She wouldn't. He hit her." My mouth fell. Jack looked tense and about to hit something. A nerve bulged in his neck. He wouldn't look me in the eyes. "My mom was so shocked. Then as he went to swing at her again I told him to stop...and he hit me. As I started to yell and tried getting my mom out of there he got up and started hitting me." I looked down at his hands clenched tightly into fist in the sheets. My heart pounded. "The next day I told my mom she needed to kick him out. She wouldn't. She said it was one night and it wouldn't happen again. Luckily she didn't get hurt as bad as me. I stayed home that day and when Scott woke up he said he was sorry. He came in and told me he was drunk and it wouldn't happen again. It did. The next week, he came back drunk and falling over. The next time he wasn't drunk. He hit my mom again for nothing. When I saw, I was so mad I wanted to kill him. He was stronger." His voice was so low I had to listen intently. "I can't stop him. Almost every weekend he hits me. I rather it be me than my mom."

"Why won't she kick him out?" I almost yelled. He shook his head.

"He threatened her. He said that if she kicks him out he will kill both of us." Tears were stinging my eyes. I was clenching the blanket now. "He gave me these last weekend for not taking out the trash," he said, raising his shirt to show the bruise I had seen before. My lungs didn't have any air in them.

"Why don't you call the cops? He's abusing you!" I said beating my hand against the bed. He shook his head.

"We can't. If we do, we don't have any proof that he's beating me. They know my criminal record and they'd think I got into a fight with a kid from school." He shrugged.

"Jack...," I said almost crying. He looked at me.

"He's never sober but I try to stay out of the house. I try to get my mom out, too, but she doesn't want to make him mad by not being at home when he is. I wanted to leave. Just move back home. Her and I. But she wouldn't. She says she 'loves him'." He rolled his eyes but you could see that they were sad. The anger. I looked down at his chest where his shirt revealed the bruise his mom's boyfriend gave him. How could he let this happen? Suddenly I was mad at him. Why can't he fight back? Why can't he take his mom and just leave! Instead of staying and getting beat up! Then I was mad at Jane: for letting this happen to her son, for letting her son get beat up by her boyfriend.

"That's why you didn't want me to come over this Saturday." I whispered. He looked up and nodded. How could I have not seen this? Why didn't I see? I could have helped him. I could have let him stay here with me. "Why is your mom letting this happen?" I finally asked. He shrugged.

"Don't get me wrong, she hates seeing me get the ass knocked out of me. It's just that she's afraid. I got into a fight with her tonight about moving again. That's why I asked to come over here." I nodded. "Plus Mr. Oversize Pants threatened if I didn't leave the house tonight he was going to give me a punch in the face." My jaw clenched. I hated this Scott guy more than I have hated anyone in my life. I almost imagined myself killing him. He put Jack through all of this! He hurt him. Jack snorted. "I slept in my car a couple times because of him. I mean I love my car but those seats are uncomfortable, but it's better than getting another bruise."

"How long has this been going on for?" I asked. He looked at his hands his jaw still tense.

"A month and a couple of weeks." I swallowed, staring at him as he looked away, avoiding my eyes. "Why didn't you tell me earlier?" I whispered. He looked up, angry.

"Like you would even care!" he growled and stood up, turning his back to me. "It's humiliating. Not being able to fight back," he whispered. I stood up, my legs shaky.

"Jack," I said, coming up to his back. I pulled at his forearm, turning him around to face me. I looked him in the eyes. "We might not be together for real and may not be the best of friends, but I care about something like that." Just tell him Lidia! No! Yes! No, I can't. He looked at me. I could feel him almost looking into my soul again. Knowing me, for who I am. "You can always stay here if you need to. I am always here for you." I said and gave his arm a squeeze.

"Thanks," he said quietly, almost in a daze. I put my arms around his waist and hugged him. He was a little shocked at first but he eventually put his arms around me and hugged me tightly back. "I think we can count ourselves as friends," he mumbled close to my ear as he put his head down to my hair. I laughed a little. I didn't want to let go. His smell was so familiar and I wanted him. No, I didn't! Yes, you do. No, I don't! I argued with myself. His warm body felt good against mine and I stuffed my face into his shoulder as much as possible. I wanted his bittersweet smell to rub off on me. Finally, we pulled back and stood awkwardly. I laughed.

"Well, um, thanks for telling me."

"You can't tell anyone, Lidia," he said, panic in his voice. I wanted to call the cops. I wanted to tell someone so they could take Scott away but Jack would hate me. I nodded.

"OK," I looked down. "Wait," I said looking up. "Will he hurt me on Saturday?" I asked, feeling scared. His eyes blazed.

"No. I won't let him. I will kill him before he touches you." He sounded so serious it almost scared me.

"What should I do? I mean, what if he finds out that I know?" I said. Jack shook his head.

"He won't hurt you, and if he finds out...," he trailed off and swallowed.

"Oh, Jack," I said, feeling tears again.

"He can't hurt you! Not for me!" Jack smirked down at me, which surprised me.

"What?" I asked. He shook his head and laughed. "This is not a laughing matter!" I yelled. He put his hand over my mouth and I stopped.

"You sound like a really freaked out girlfriend afraid that her boyfriend is going to die." I raised an eyebrow and he pulled his hand back. I shrugged and looked down.

"I am," I whispered.

"Just don't say anything about it and stay close to me." I nodded. "And my mom said he might not even come. Depends." Relief filled me. I don't want Jack to get beat up because of me. It wasn't right. I would call the cops if he did.

"OK," I said and looked at the clock. "It's midnight already," I said with a sigh. He nodded.

"We should probably go to bed." I went back to my bed and put away my books. "You read?" he asked, surprised. I looked at him and showed him the book. He raised an eyebrow. "Lord of the Flies, a little gory for a bedtime story?" he asked, amused. I laughed but then stopped and looked at him.

"You read it before?" This time he laughed and lay down on the floor.

"I'm not as dumb as I look, Princess." I shrugged.

"You don't seem the type."

"And you shouldn't judge."

I narrowed my eyes at him and climbed in under the covers.

"I wasn't judging…it's just…"

"Yeah, you were," he said.

"OK, so I was!" I said. "But can you blame me? I mean Jack Walker reading? Really, I would think hell would freeze over before that happened."

He chuckled.

"I read. I read a lot, actually," he said quietly. I turned off the light and just the light streaming through the window from the street came in. It cast an orange glow.

"Mm, you know I'm a little worried about you?" I said, leaning over the edge of the bed where he was. He had his hands behind his head and not under his Barbie cover, just lying on top with his clothes on. He looked up at me and my pulse started to beat faster.

"Why?" he asked. I smiled a little.

"Because you're always doing things I would never have expected." My words were soft and sweet and they meant a lot. He smiled without showing his white teeth. "Goodnight," I whispered.

"Night."

I lay back in bed and pulled a pillow to me and closed my eyes, smiling. Even though everything with Jack was on my mind, I couldn't get that smile out of my brain. Or the fact that he was sleeping on the floor a foot away from me.

Chapter 28

I woke up to my alarm clock going off. Jack and I both groaned. I slapped it off and put my face back into the pillow. 'Why couldn't it be Saturday?' I thought to myself. I want to sleep in! I sat up and yanked my hair out of the pony tail and let the curls fall down around my shoulders.

"I think my parents left," I mumbled. Jack grunted in response. I stood up and went to my dresser, pulling out a pair of jeans and a pretty shirt. "I'll be back," I muttered and left the room. I went to the bathroom and changed quickly, brushing my hair out and putting on a little makeup. I grabbed my clothes and went back into my room. Jack was still sleeping. I smirked. I threw my clothes in the corner and went over to him. He was laying on his stomach with his brown locks covering his face. I leaned down, my legs on either side of him. "Jack?" I coed. "Get up." I grinned as I thought of a plan. I grabbed the pillow off my bed and stood up. "Waky waky," I muttered and went to throw the pillow down on his face when he jumped up scaring me. He grabbed my waist and pushed me back onto the mattress. I screamed and laughed as he landed on top of me. His blue eyes were still a little sleepy but his lips curved up into a grin. "You're a rat," I said, laughing.

"And you were going to hit me with a pillow," he said, sounding insulted. I giggled. He laughed and got off of me. Not like I wanted him to, though. He put out his hand after ruffling his hair. I took it and he pulled me up. I laughed and fixed my shirt. "Can I use the shower?" he asked.

I nodded.

"Yeah, go ahead."

He nodded and grabbed his backpack and headed into the bathroom. I heard the shower start as I grabbed a pop-tart and headed back to the room. Not too long after, he got out and came back into the room wearing dark jeans and a red T-shirt. He smelled good too. His hair was wet and fell down in front of his eyes. It was hard not to stare but I averted my eyes to my finger nails.

"Mm, a pop-tart," he said and took it from me.

"Hey!" I yelled. He sat down beside me on the bed and I felt drips of water land on my arms and face. "That's mine," I said as he took another bite out of it. It was half way in his mouth already.

"What are you talking about, girl? You don' need it." I gasped and he laughed, almost choking on the pop-tart. He pulled it out of his mouth as I hit his shoulder and he laughed.

"Dork," I muttered. At least I had eaten the other one. He finished it off and sighed.

"I'm still hungry," he mumbled.

"Oh, poor baby," I said and stood up, already dizzy from his cologne. "We've got school, mister." He nodded.

"Let's skip," he said, putting his hands behind his head.

"Ugh, no." I said as a matter-of-fact. "Did you even bring any of your books along?" I asked looking at his old backpack.

"Nope, I leave them at school."

"Don't you have homework?" I asked. He looked at me and smirked.

"Yep!"

I rolled my eyes.

"I wish we could but—"

"Why can't we?"

I looked at him, scrunching my nose up while thinking.

"My parents would kill me," I said. "Especially if we leave the house—"

"We don't have to," he said. I looked at him with knitted brows.

"You've done this before haven't you?"

"A million times."

"Figured." I looked up at the corner of my room and sighed.

"Fine," I said, giving in. Jack grinned. I put my backpack back down and jumped into bed beside Jack, putting my hands behind my head and staring up at my ceiling. "So, what now?" I asked. I felt him shrug beside me. It was silent as we thought.

"Ooh!" he said and jumped up. He turned and looked down at me, grinning.

"What?" I asked.

"Smallville is back to back all day on demand."

I grinned.

"I think we found a plan."

I thought for a moment.

"What's wrong?" he asked. I looked at him.

"We need food."

He nodded smiling.

"Agreed." He was staring at me now. His eyes drifted from my eyes, down to my neck, then my chest then to my stomach and finally landing on the bare skin showing around my hip. His chest heaved a little. I realized we were in an uncomfortable position and sat up real quick, bringing my top down. I cleared my throat.

"Um, let's go to the '7 Eleven' down the road and get some snacks." He nodded and cleared his head. 'See Lidia, all he's looking for is sex and someone to hook up with. I'm sure he's had sex before. He seems like he has but maybe that's just a cover up. Of course he did it with Kendra! She bragged about it!' I sighed to myself. Don't let him do this to you. I'm sure he looked like that when Kendra was lying around the house in her thong and bra! I got to my feet and went to my dresser.

"I've got some money we can spend." I grabbed two twenties and turned to Jack making a smile come to my lips even though my mind was showing me pictures of Kendra and Jack together....doing something that I had no experience with. "Let's go."

Chapter 29

I drove quickly to the '7 Eleven' and walked in. I went straight to the ice cream section and looked around, holding my keys in my hand.

"Ice cream," Jack said behind me. I nodded.

"Yes, a big box," I confirmed. I smiled as I saw mint chocolate chip. I opened the door and grabbed it. "Which one do you want?" I asked. He looked over my shoulder, trying to choose.

"Rocky Road," he said. I grabbed it. I shut the door and felt the cold ice prickle the skin on my fingers. He had two bags of chips and a bottle of Mountain Dew.

"You know me so well." He smirked. We paid for our stuff and headed back. We put our junk food on the coffee table and Jack searched and found Smallville on the T.V. as I grabbed some blankets and threw them on the sofa with us. I pulled one around me and started to eat my box of ice cream with a large spoon.

"Here we go," Jack said as he found season 5 of Smallville.

"Wait. Let's start from the beginning." I said. He sighed.

"They only have seasons 5 to 7." I frowned and he laughed.

"Fine, okay." He got his box of ice cream and propped his feet up on the coffee table and I smiled, remembering the time we fought and landed on each other.

"Man, he is such a hunk!" I gushed as Aqua man jumped out of the water along with Lois without a shirt on.

"Lidia!" Jack yelled, laughing. "I do not want to know that." He shuddered. I laughed.

"Why? Look at those abs! I mean come on! Only he can look like that." Jack frowned playfully.

"I have those abs. Want to see?" he asked. I shook my head laughing. He put down his half empty box of ice cream and pulled his shirt up. He sucked in his gut and flexed. I burst out laughing. He did look good but I wasn't about to tell him that. "What?" he yelled. I fell back onto the sofa laughing hard.

"Those are nothing!" I said pointing to his stomach. He laughed.

"Not yet."

I rolled my eyes and settled down. I took a chip and put it in my mouth. I looked at Jack's half empty box of Rocky Road.

"Before you eat it all, I want a taste." I said. He took a big mouthful and smiled at me the spoon sticking out of his mouth. I rolled my eyes.

"I want a taste of yours too," he said. I grabbed my box and spooned a big bite.

"Here," he pulled the spoon out of his mouth and filled it with the chocolate rocky road.

"Aren't you like disgusted by eating off the same spoon as me?" he asked. I laughed and shook my head.

"I could care less. I've already swapped spit with you." He wiggled his eye brows.

"Speaking of swapping spit, do you want to make out?"

I laughed and shoved my spoon into his mouth. He choked a little, but ate it. He put his spoon in my mouth and I ate the Rocky Road.

"Mm, not bad," I said.

"Yours isn't either." I smirked. He laughed and I frowned.

"What?" I asked.

"You've got ice cream on your chin." I wiped my chin and blushed a little. He laughed more. I nudged him and he nudged me back. I slapped his leg and he pushed me over. I rammed my elbow in his ribs. I laughed as he coughed and grunted.

"Oh my gosh!" I yelled terrified. I looked at him as he held his chest. "Oh, I'm so, so, sorry I totally forgot about—."

"It's fine," he laughed and rubbed his rib. "You're good." I smiled but felt worried.

"Seriously, I didn't mean to."

"I know you didn't," he said calmly. I felt bad and gave him a sad smile. He returned it with a dorky grin. "You can't hit that hard, anyhow."

I rolled my eyes.

"I would punch you again but it might hurt even worse."

He laughed. "Nah, it takes a lot for me to get hurt that bad." I didn't like the way he said it. I didn't want him to talk about getting hurt. It made me angry. I sighed. It was only noon, so we had two hours if not more. Our attention went back to the TV and I drummed my fingers on the sofa, deciding. I clucked my tongue and looked at Jack. He was about to eat a chip when he saw me looking at him. I wiggled my eye brows. He raised one.

"I'm bored. Let's make out." He half smiled and put the chip down. He looked at me and smirked as he leaned over and kissed me. It was good. So, so, so good. He pulled back a little and teased my lips. I rolled my eyes. "So, this doesn't affect our friendship or anything?" I made sure, pulling back a little. He nodded, his eyes closed, feeling for my lips again. "Just to have fun right?" He nodded again and kissed me lightly.

"Since we're not getting anywhere with Kendra or Grant," said Jack as he touched my lips again. I nodded too.

"Might as well get something out of it," I mumbled, kissing his top lip. I was feeling it again. The butterflies in my stomach and the heat in my lower stomach. The gentleness of his lips. His hands came up and rested on my neck softly. I kissed the side of his lips pulling back and then kissing him again on his bottom lip. I pulled back enough to get air. "Screw it, since we're going to do this, we might as well do it right," I said and pulled him on top of me on the sofa. He laughed a throaty laugh as he pulled himself a little off me to avoid hurting me. The sofa was nice and comfortable with soft blankets under my fingertips. I put my hands on his waist and pulled him down closer to me. I wanted him so much closer. He groaned in his throat and his other hand was on my waist. We were kissing just lightly. Our hearts were already beating loudly. My body was craving more than just kisses, but I couldn't let anything more happen. I deepened the kiss and he got the idea. I tasted the chocolate on his lips and he winced when I pressed too hard and hurt his cut lip. I pulled back slightly but he just came down harder on me. Which wasn't bad, of course, but I didn't want to hurt him. I put my tongue in his mouth and ran it across his. It woke up and twirled with mine. I felt like moaning but I knew that wouldn't help just making out. He pulled back and kissed my chin. Then down a little, then down a little more. He sucked right below my ear where you could feel my pulsing heartbeat. I gasped. My fingers grabbed his back and I arched my body to his. I pulled my hands up quick to him and pulled his head back up to my lips. "Just here," I whispered and I could feel him smiling. That was my spot. Grant never found that before. I put my hands in Jack's hair and kept kissing him slowly.

Chapter 30

We made out for a long time. But it felt so fast. Before I knew it I heard the clock in the dining room going off. I pulled back with my lips feeling swollen.

"What time is it?" I asked, panic in my voice. Jack jumped off of me and looked at the time. "3:00 p.m.!" he said, shocked. I jumped up.

"Damn-it! My mom is going to be home any minute now and look at this!" The coffee table was a mess with junk food and chips. The sofa was a mess too. If she saw this, she'll know we skipped. Jack looked me in the eyes and knew the same thing. We quickly grabbed all the junk food and put it away. Then cleaned the table and put the melted ice cream away. I folded all the blankets and laid them neatly on the sofa. I turned back to Jack with a sigh. "Okay, done." At that we heard a car pull in. Jack and I ran to the window to see my mom getting out of her car. "Um," I thought for a moment. "Upstairs!" I yelled and we both ran up. I slammed my door just as the front door opened. I grabbed my Algebra book and we jumped onto the bed.

"Lidia?" Mom came into the room.

"So if you do this and divide—oh, hey, Mom," I said, looking up. Jack smiled up at her.

"You guys are home early."

"Um, school let out a little early for the play." She nodded.

"Oh, OK. What play is it?" My mouth opened a little.

"Um...Hamlet!" I said. She smiled.

"Oh I love that book! Maybe we could go see it—."

"No!" I yelled. She jumped and frowned. "I mean...you can't. It's just that this play is only for...um...for the parents of the kids!" She nodded.

"Okay, fine. Jack, are you staying for supper?" she asked.

"Actually, I should probably head home soon," he said, sounding a little worried.

"Oh OK, well come say bye before you leave." Mom left the room and I sighed and threw my book back on the ground.

"That was close," Jack laughed. "Well, Princess, it's not like this wasn't fun but I think my mom is probably really worried about me right now. I turned off my cell so she probably called like a million times." I nodded and bit at my lip.

"Do you think you'll be OK?" I whispered. He sighed and looked at me.

"I'm not sure. I guess we'll see." I frowned.

"Maybe you should stay here. I mean we're going back to your house tomorrow evening anyhow." He smiled sadly at me.

"I really need to go home, Lidia."

I nodded and looked up. "Just call me when you get back, okay?"

He grinned. "Worried about me?"

I blushed a little. "A little."

He smiled. It was sweet.

"I'll be fine," he said. He kissed my hair and stood up. "I'll call you tonight," he confirmed as he grabbed his bag. I waved as he left my room. I heard his car start up noisily then drive away. I really hoped he'd be alright. Maybe Scott decided to leave for good. I sighed. I blushed a little as I remembered us on the sofa.

A little while later I heard my phone going off. I grabbed it out of my jeans and answered it. "Lidia, hey," Jack said sweetly.

"Hey," I smiled.

"I have some good news."

"Yeah?" I asked. He lowered his voice.

"Scott isn't coming tomorrow. I think my mom said he was busy." I sighed. Relief washing over me.

"Good." Then a thought occurred to me. "Did he...?" I trailed off not wanting to say it. Jack knew what I was talking about.

"No, he only stayed a little when I came back but he left and didn't say a word to me." I nodded to myself. Good, he didn't hurt him. "Well, I better hit the hay. I'm beat!" I laughed.

"From stuffing your face with ice cream?" I asked. He chuckled.

"No! What are you talking about? We were working' our brains out at school, remember?" I laughed.

"Yeah, I remember."

"Night, Lidia," he whispered. I lay down on the bed and smiled.

"Night." I hung up and sighed. Maybe this wouldn't turn out bad after all. But then maybe it would.

Chapter 31

I slept in, happy that it was a Saturday and then got up at 2:00 p.m. Mom and dad were watching TV in the living room. I was stunned to see them together but then they were trying to fix their marriage. "Hey," I said. Mom smiled.

"Sleep long enough?" she asked. I laughed.

"Yeah." I sat down beside her and saw dad texting someone on his phone. Some things never change. "Um, Mom, did I tell you that I was going to Jack's tonight to have supper with his mom?" I said looking at her. She smiled.

"If you did, I can't remember." I almost rolled my eyes but didn't.

"OK, well, Jane is making stuff and invited me over. So, Jack is picking me up at about 6 but I'm not sure by what time we'll be back." She nodded.

"Okay, that's fine." I got up and got something to eat and started to read Lord of the Flies.

It was 5 p.m. when I took a hot shower and got dressed in the red and white polka-dot dress that I had hidden in the back of my closet. I smiled. This was supposed to be for Grant. But maybe I got it for someone else, not Grant…maybe I knew I had feelings for---.

"Lidia!" Dad called from outside the bathroom door, scaring me. "I need to get in there for a second. Are you almost done?" I sighed and slipped the dress on.

"Yeah, hold on a minute." It came just two inches above my knees. Good thing I had a long coat. My coat was just as long as the dress, so it would keep me warm. I opened the door and grabbed my stuff. He smiled.

"Sorry," I rolled my eyes and went into my room. I combed out my hair that I had dried and left down. It tumbled a little below my shoulders. Not too long like all the people have now, but not too short either. It was a little wavy, so I curled a few pieces and put on my flats. I heard the car from a mile away.

"Lidia! Jack's here!" Mom called. I sighed and checked myself in the mirror. I didn't put on a lot of makeup. Just a little. I smiled and the girl in the mirror smiled back. This is me, I guess. Someone in between a roughy-toughy girl and the girlie-girl. Perfect. I grabbed my coat, keys and cell phone, not bothering to get a purse. They were pointless. I ran down the stairs as Jack came in.

"Mrs. Taylor," Jack said sweetly to mom. She blushed.

"Please call me Jill." He nodded. Jack looked....really handsome. He was wearing dark jeans with a button up dark green shirt and his leather jacket. He was wearing a brown skull hat that almost matched his hair. I came down the stairs and quickly slipped in.

"I'm ready," I said, behind my mom. Jack's eyes shifted over to me. His eyes had that look that I could never figure out. His eyes were locked on me. He looked like he was stunned where he was. I smiled lightly. Those blue eyes. Why did they make me blush so much? Why could he see everything in me?

"Oh Lidia! You look so pretty!" Mom said and gave me a hug.

"Thanks, Mom," I said and pulled back. I looked at Jack again who tried to regain his composure but was failing.

"Yeah you look..." He trailed off and looked down, blushing a little. I smiled kindly.

"Mom, I'll be back when I can."

"Oh, just have fun!" she said and smiled. I nodded.

"See ya, dad!" I yelled.

"Bye!" he yelled from his office. I walked towards Jack and he looked up at me from in between his lashes.

"Come on, buddy," I said and nudged him playfully. He smiled and we walked out the door. "So, what is your Mom making for supper?" I asked as we drove out of the parking lot.

"Um, I'm not sure. But she is going totally crazy, rushing around making stuff." I laughed.

"Aw, that's sweet." It was silent.

"She really likes you, Lidia," Jack said and looked over at me with a small smile. I smiled.

"I think she's great, too."

He looked back at the road and put his arm beside mine and they touched. We didn't move back. We left our elbows touching. I wanted it. I wanted to be able to touch him no matter what. If it was just the elbows, I would be okay. And no, I wasn't going to object to that. I'm not going to argue because it was the truth. I still wasn't sure what I felt for Jack...and I was worried about that. Because in the end, I would probably get my heart broken.

Chapter 32

We got to the house and quickly ran to the door. We walked up the stairs slowly. I thought Jack was going to say something but he just looked up. But, then I felt a hand come into mine. We intertwined our fingers and I smiled. We got up to his floor and he unlocked the door. He looked back at me and smiled a crooked smile.

"Be prepared. She's going all out."

I laughed and nodded. He opened the door and the smell of baked bread morphed from the room. We walked in and Jack shut the door, not bothering to lock it.

"Mom! We're here!" he called. We walked into the kitchen and smoke came up from the stove as Jane pulled a pan off. She looked up and grinned. She was wearing a nice black dress that made her look like a teenager. But still mom-approvable.

"Lidia!" she said and gave me a hug. "It's so nice to see you again!"

"You, too," I said and smiled.

"We'll I'm making food. It's almost done, so it will be a minute. Jack you go take her to the table," she said. He nodded. We walked into the living room where they had set up a table. It had candles in the middle and salad and bread sticks already on it. Jack pulled out my chair and I sat down.

"Thank you," I said, a little surprised. He nodded and took a drink of his ice water before sitting down.

"Like I said, she went all out," he whispered. I laughed.

"It's okay. She did a great job."

"Damn-it!" she yelled.

"Mom! Are you okay?" Jack asked, half laughing.

"Yeah! Yeah! I'm fine!" she called back. He laughed. A little while later she came out with a tray of spaghetti covered in sauce.

"Mm, it smells good," I said. She grinned.

"Good! I hope it's as good as it looks," she mumbled as she sat down with a sigh. She smiled at Jack and me from her end of the small table. "OK let's give thanks." She bowed her head. "Jack?" she asked. He sighed and gave a quick prayer. She smiled as she put her napkin on her lap. "So, how are you Lidia?" I took a bread stick.

"I'm pretty good. It's just that school has been a pain and stuff." She nodded.

"Are you going to college after high school?" she asked. I nodded.

"Yeah I want to go to college in California. There's a really good one there that's affordable." She smiled. Jack passed me the spaghetti and I scooped some onto my plate.

"What do you want to major in?"

I thought for a moment as I twirled my spaghetti around my fork.

"I want to be a doctor." She raised an eyebrow surprised.

"Really?" I nodded.

"It's always been my dream, I guess." I shrugged. "My Mom isn't too helpful, though," I said and ate a mouthful of spaghetti. She frowned.

"Why not? It's a great job! If went to college, I would have done something like that." I sighed.

"My mom is a very...well there really isn't a word for her. She wants me in a pageant and to be the next Ms. America." Jack choked on his food but quickly swallowed and retained himself from laughing. I narrowed my eyes at him just as he grinned at me. I rolled my eyes. "I'm something she isn't, so she isn't very supportive of me wanting to be a doctor. How come you didn't go to college?" I asked. She sighed.

"Well, my ex-husband and I were high school sweethearts." I smiled. "And we got married right out of high school. It wasn't a year before Jack was born and we couldn't afford for me to go to college after." I frowned slightly.

"And your ex-husband, what did he do?" She ate a bite of her food before answering.

"He worked with his brother as lawyers." I nodded. "But after he left I had to get a job to take care of Jack." I looked down and took a drink of water.

"Did you ever think about going back to school now?" I asked looking up. I saw Jack stop eating. Jane smiled kindly at me.

"I don't think I could."

"Why not?" Jack asked putting down his fork. Jane bit her lip. "We could get some extra cash." Jack suggested. I smiled at him.

"Oh I don't—."

"I think you should," I said. She smiled.

"I never thought about it...but now I will." She ate, looking happy.

"Mom, maybe—." Jack was cut off as the front door banged open. We all jumped and turned. A middle-aged man with brown hair stood at the door. His eyes were almost black.

"Jane," he said, the word cold and cruel. Jack's whole body went rigid. I stared at the man.

"Oh...Scott," Jane said, standing up and pushing down her skirt.

"What's this?" he asked. He was a tall, big man. Jack's hands were clenched in a fist, mine mimicked his. This was Scott. She went over and he pulled her in to kiss him. He pulled her away quickly.

"We were just having dinner," she said her voice a little shaky.

"And, you didn't tell me?" he asked.

"No! No, no, sweetie. We were waiting for you." He nodded. He looked at me and my jaw clenched.

"Hi," he said, his voice becoming gentler. "Who's this?" he asked. Jack stood up his hands still clenched in fists at his sides.

"She's my girlfriend," Jack said, his voice deep. Scott raised an eyebrow but looked bored.

"Didn't know you even had a girl," he said. Scott ignored him and smiled creepily at me. "I'm Scott."

"Lidia," I answered back, trying to unclench my teeth.

"Well Jane, I want something to eat, so why don't you set me up a plate?" She nodded and ran into the kitchen. Jack sat back down his body tense and ready to pounce. I put my hand on his leg and he flinched but then saw me. I calmed him down with my eyes. It was OK. He wasn't going to hurt any of us. If I just behave and if he likes me, he might not hurt Jack. But this guy was a creep. I could see that. Every time I looked at him I could see him punching Jack. I wanted to punch Scott myself. He dragged a chair over to the table in front of me and sat down. I got a whiff of a heavy alcohol and cigarettes. "So, how long have you been dating?" he asked, putting his lazy arm on the back of the chair. Jack didn't eat.

"A month or two now," I answered. He nodded, looking at me. I stared back at him, showing him that I wasn't scared.

"Okay, here," Jane said, coming back into the room and putting the plate down. He filled it with spaghetti and breadsticks. Jane sat down and started to eat again.

"How was your day?" Jane asked Scott. He shrugged.

"Same, same."

Jane nodded and took a drink of her water. It was quiet and I ate a little more but didn't really feel like eating. I was still tense with Scott across from me who I could tell was watching me a lot. It was creepy.

"Are you mute?" Scott asked Jack. Jack looked over at Scott and glared.

"No."

Scott laughed.

"Your girl here is going to get bored with you if you don't watch out."

Jack clenched his teeth. I wanted badly to hold his hand but they were clenched too tightly together.

"No, I don't think I will," I said boldly. Scott switched his eyes over to me and I almost gulped. They looked black. No soul.

"Mm," he said and started eating again. I swallowed a little and took a drink of water. "Do we have any beer?" Scott asked Jane. Jane looked up, her eyes a little big.

"N-no I forgot to get some." He rolled his eyes.

"Jane!" he yelled. Jack moved a little toward him, his hands ready to punch but stopped. Jane looked scared.

"I'm sorry I forgot. I'll get——."

"No! It's fine. I'll go get some tonight," he muttered coldly. He mumbled something that sounded like 'worthless'. I gritted my teeth together wanting badly to yell. How could Jack not hurt this guy? He was a total asshole! Jane stood up and picked up her stuff.

"I'm going to wash up the plates," she said calmly, but her voice wavered.

"Good," Scott muttered but then smiled at me. "She can be that way sometimes, just ignore her." My mouth almost dropped a little. He was apologizing for Jane? She didn't do anything! "The game's on," Scott said and stood up. He drank down his water in disgust and then flipped himself down on the sofa and switched on the TV. I stood up.

"I'm going to help your mom," I whispered. Jack stood up, too, and grabbed some of the plates and cups.

"OK." I took the plates and walked in. Jane stood at the sink, washing.

"Here," I said and set them down by the sink.

"Oh, thank you," she said.

"Can I help?" I asked. She smiled gratefully.

"That would be wonderful." I rinsed and put them on the dish rack. I put the spaghetti in a box and put it in the fridge. "You're a real help. Thank you." Jane said kindly. I smiled and rinsed more.

"Yeah, no problem. We have a dish washer and I don't get to do this kind of stuff. My mom only cooks once in a while and she doesn't do dishes."

She laughed until her eyes wrinkled at the sides into crow's feet. But they were sweet.

"Well, I know a lot about washing dishes."

I laughed.

"You're really good for Jack, you know that?" she said, looking over at me. I smiled sadly. "I'm so glad he found a girl. And you are the perfect match for him." My heart was almost tearing. Too bad I wasn't that girl. Too bad he doesn't feel that way for me.

"Thanks," I whispered. She laughed.

"He needs a woman to put him in his place!"

I laughed.

"Yeah." Jack came in and leaned on the counter, his teeth still clenched, but less tense. I looked at him and mouthed, 'Are you OK?' He nodded stiffly. I gave him a reassuring smile.

Chapter 33

Jane and I talked at the table and told stories. It was nice because I didn't even notice Scott. Jack stood, leaned on the wall behind me, watching Scott out of the corner of his eye.

"Oh, wow," Jane said, leaning back on her chair, smiling.

"What time is it?" I asked.

"It's 10:00 p.m."

I laughed.

"Wow, um, Jack we should probably get back to my house. My parents didn't give me a time but I'm sure they'll yell if it's too late." He nodded. I stood up and Jane did, too.

"Thank you for coming over."

I smiled.

"Thank you for having me." She gave me a tight hug.

"I want her to come back," Jane said, letting me go and talking to Jack. He smiled lightly.

"OK, Mom," he said.

"Be safe!" she called as we went out the door. The stairs were cold, so I wrapped my coat around me tighter. We headed to the car and got in quickly when we saw a group of guys walking from one end of the street. It was silent as we went over the bridge.

"So, that's Scott," I stated more than questioned.

"Yeah...he wasn't supposed to come. But of course the idiot can't stay away for more than-."

"Jack!" I said. "It's OK. As long as he doesn't hurt you, we're OK." He glanced over at me and looked away quickly.

"I wasn't worried about getting hurt...I was worried he was going to hurt you," he mumbled softly. I looked at him. His jaw was tight but I swear I could see pink running to his cheeks. I smiled and laughed lightly. I took his hand and brought it up to my lip, kissed it and patted his hand.

"I can take care of myself there, Mr. Walker. If he would ever try to hurt me, I would just open up a can of 'Whoop Ass!'." He laughed. We got to the house and I got out. He walked me up the stairs talking about some concert Jane took him to.

"ACDC?" I asked surprised. He nodded and laughed.

"My mom loves them," he said.

"So, that's why 'Back in Black!' is your ring tone." He laughed.

"Yeah."

I smiled.

"You're really good to your mom," I said. He sighed but smiled. "I'll see you on Monday." I started for the door.

"Wait!" he said quickly. I turned around as Jack came up and kissed my cheek lightly.

"You look beautiful," he whispered. Shivers ran down my spine. With that, he turned and went back down the steps and got in his car. I smiled and went inside. I heard the car drive away and sighed. Dad was in the living room watching the game when I walked in.

"I'm going to bed," I said. He nodded. I went up to my room, slipping off my shoes and jacket. I pulled off my dress and got into bed, not feeling like changing. I got my book and started to read, almost in a daze.

Sunday morning, I went downstairs and finished my book. I sighed as dad flipped the channels on the TV. I need a book. I looked at my phone and sighed. No texts from Jack.

"Dad," I said standing up.

"Mm?" he asked.

"I'm going to go to the library quick okay?" He nodded.

"Be careful out there, though. It's getting a little icy." I nodded and grabbed my coat, scarf and my gloves. Mom came into the living room getting a magazine off the coffee stand.

"I need something to read while we're there," she mumbled. I headed out the door and ran to my car as I felt the icy breeze. It was going to snow this week. I could tell. I got to the library and went to my favorite section. I moved my fingers across the leather backs and read the last names. I smiled as I pulled out a dusty Mice and Men. It was a tiny book but it was so good. I'd already read it a couple times. I then moved to the next isle and found Stephen King. I smiled as I pulled out a large book with a couple stories in it. I went around the other corner thinking maybe one more book would be good. There was a table in the corner and there was Grant sitting at it. I stopped, frozen, and went to step back around the corner when he saw me.

"Lidia!" he said, surprised. I looked up and smiled.

"Hey, Grant." He motioned me over. I awkwardly went over.

"So, what are you doing here?" he asked.

I laughed. "Getting books?"

He smiled. "Sorry, stupid question."

I nodded.

"Are you studying?" I asked.

He sighed. "Yep, history." He tapped his pencil and nodded. "It sucks."

I rolled my eyes.

"You were never good at that subject."

He laughed. "Yeah, not my best."

It was silent. I shifted awkwardly on my feet.

"Well, I better get going," I said and headed down the aisle.

"Um, yeah…okay bye!" he called after me.

"Bye," I said and walked to check out my books. "Awkward," I muttered.

Chapter 34

I went home that night and read one of my books by the fireplace while dad watched TV and mom drank a glass of white wine. She sipped and filled up again. This happened over and over again. I shook my head and got into the book I was reading. The next thing I knew, Dad and Mom were sleeping and I was alone with the blazing fire. I smiled as I smelled the fresh wood burning. Christmas. That's what I thought. Christmas. I realized that it was in two and a half weeks. For about 4 years now we hadn't put anything up but a stupid Christmas tree we got on Christmas Eve. I bit at my lip as I looked up the stairs. Could I? I smiled and put my book down. I quickly ran up the stairs and into the attic. I grabbed the dusty boxes of decorations and ran down stairs, tip-toeing as I went past Mom and Dad's door. I curved lights around the stair case and put little Santas everywhere. I set fake snow and a manger set on the piano. I hung up our old stockings above the fireplace and smiled. They were torn at the edges. I had made them when I was about 3 or 4 with Mom. I put my hands on my hips and looked around the room. It looked like a Christmas castle. It smelled of cinnamon and musk. But that's how I liked it. I made a cup of hot chocolate and sat back down with my book. I glanced out the window and smiled as I saw it clouding over. Maybe we wouldn't have any school tomorrow. I grinned even more. I checked my phone and frowned seeing that I didn't have a text or message from Jack. I was about to write him, then thought better. Maybe he was busy. Remember, you're not his real girlfriend. How many times have I reminded myself?

My alarm went off and I groaned and slapped it off. I looked at my blinking cell phone and snatched it off the table and looked. Text message from Candice. I pressed my lips together and sighed. I stood up and took a shower which took a little longer than usual. I got dressed in warm clothes and went downstairs. Mom was packing stuff into a bag from the cupboard. Stuff looking like liquor bottles.

"Honey!" Mom said with a smile.

"Are you guys leaving this morning?" I asked. She nodded.

"Ugh! How much stuff can you pack?" my dad mumbled as he came down the stairs holding 4 suitcases. I rolled my eyes at Mom.

"What? It's just a few things." I laughed. She got her bag and I helped them carry their stuff to the car. I put it in the back as the wind whipped at me and I shivered. Mom sighed as Dad shut the back. "Well that's it," Mom smiled at me. "Come here." She pulled me into a hug and I smelled her peach hair. "I love you, sweetie." I nodded. "There's money in the jar. If you want to go shopping, the credit cards are on the counter. Call Mrs. Rogers if you have any trouble or just give us a ring. But we probably won't pick up," she grinned at my dad, who blushed a little. I raised an eyebrow.

"I don't want to know," I muttered. She giggled.

"And no boys after midnight okay?" I rolled my eyes.

"Yeah, I know that." She nodded.

"That's my girl." She got into the car as Dad gave me a hug and said to be safe.

"Oh!" he said turning before he got in. "There's supposed to be a bad storm tonight and into tomorrow, so be safe on your way home from school." I smiled.

"I will." He gave me a salute and I laughed and did it back. They drove off as I waved. I sighed and went back inside and got my bag for school. I looked outside, waiting for Jack. I tapped my foot as the clock got closer to the time I was supposed to be at school. I finally got out my cell and called Jack.

"Hey, this is Jack…leave—."

"Damn-it!" I muttered as I realized his phone was off. I stopped and frowned. I didn't remember him ever letting it go dead. I bit at my lip not sure what to do. I looked back out the window knowing if I didn't leave now, I would be late. I groaned and stomped my feet as I went out of the house, locking the door behind me. I kept looking around for him but he was nowhere. There was a churning in my stomach. Did he just take off? Did he not care anymore? Did something happen? I almost threw up again but I tried to think of other things.

On the way to school I called Jack's cell 10 times and texted him about 20 messages. I wasn't feeling good as I walked into English and still didn't see him.

"Hey!" Candice said as she waved at me while talking to one of her actors from the play. I didn't smile. "What's wrong?" she asked as she came up to me. I turned to her.

"Jack hasn't called or text me. I haven't seen him since Saturday." She frowned.

"Doesn't he always do this?" I shrugged.

"Not really." She sighed.

"Don't freak out about it, Lidia. Seriously, guys do that all the time." I nodded but wasn't so sure. No, you need to be. You know what! I bet he is out playing hooky and got a couple girls. He ditched me again! Anger rose in me and I slammed my locker door shut.

"You're probably right." She laughed.

"Well I got to go. Call me tonight so we can talk." I nodded.

"Yeah, sure. My parents left me for the week so you can come over anytime." She grinned.

"Awesome! Maybe this weekend over the holiday break." I laughed.

"Yeah, party!" She laughed and hurried on her way down the hall. I turned to go to my next class, teeth clenched, hands in fist at my sides, wanting everything to have Jack in front of me so I could hit him really hard for ditching me.

****

I got home that evening just as the snow started to fall. It was amazing, I thought. I watched a flake hit the window, then slide down it and melt. I turned on the TV and started watching the news. From what it sounded like, we were going to get a butt load! Like a foot. 'No school tomorrow!' I thought happily. I stood up and turned on the fire to make it warmer as the soft glow formed an orange light around the room. I settled back on the sofa and was channel surfing when I heard a noise. I frowned. Then before I could get up, there was a loud bang on the door, then it opened and Jack fell onto the floor, unable to get up.

Chapter 35

"Jack!" I screamed in horror as I ran over and crouched down trying to lift his face up as the cold winter air came in from the door. His face was bloody with a big wound open on his forehead. A big bruise was forming on his chin. "Oh, God, Jack," I whispered. I pushed him over trying to see him. He groaned, one of his eyes black and blue and the other was trying to open. "Jack?" I shook him, tears forming in my eyes.

"Lidia…" he mumbled.

"Yes! Yes, I'm here," I told him. He groaned, his eye brows going together.

"Come here," he whispered, trying to lift his hand. I bent lower, a couple tears falling from my eyes. "You sound really sexy when you're scared," he whispered. I jumped back and stared at him wide-eyed. He grinned but then winced when it hurt.

"You idiot! How can you joke when you're practically dying on my floor?!" I yelled.

"Ow," he mumbled closing his good eye. I stood up and shut the front door, seeing Jack's car parked in the yard. I locked the door. Oh my gosh. What happened? I had goose bumps all over. I had bad feeling about this. I sat back down on my knees, my stomach churning.

"Jack?" I whispered and put my hand on his cheek. He sighed and leaned into it not opening his eye. "You need to stand up okay?" I whispered. He didn't move. My heart was pounding. Was he dying? Should I call the ambulance? "Come on! Crack another joke. Please!" I begged. He groaned and moved his head. I stood up and pulled him to me. He was practically lying on me. "Jack, come on! Please help me," I said. Finally, I got him to the sofa and laid him down. He grunted. I was crying now. I ran to the kitchen and got a glass of water. "Jack, you need water." I pulled his head up and poured water in his mouth. He swallowed and then opened his eye a little.

"Why are you crying?" he asked. I breathed a sigh of relief. If he was talking, we would be okay.

"You. Silly." I said, shaking my head. He half smiled but it looked like it hurt.

"I'm fine...just...just give me 5 ibuprofen."

I frowned.

"You need to rest." He nodded and leaned his head on the sofa. I ran upstairs and grabbed the medicine and pulled out 5 pills. I got a cup and filled it with hot water and a wash cloth and went back downstairs. "Here," I whispered sitting on the floor next to the couch. I put the pills in his mouth and grabbed my water bottle and let him drink it down as he leaned up his head. He nodded and I pulled back. He let his head fall back down. His eyes closed. "We need to talk." I whispered. He was silent. I swallowed hard as I looked across at his chest. I slowly peeled off his jacket then was afraid to see what was under the other shirt. I saw it already traveling up to his shoulder. I slipped off his shirt as he grunted but didn't say no. I gasped and put my hand to my mouth. There was a large bruise from his stomach all the way up to his shoulder. Then on his arm were hand prints. "Oh my gosh!" I yelled. Jack looked up at me, his eyes looking distant. He gave a short laugh then coughed.

"It's just a couple of bruises."

"He did this to you, didn't he?" I whispered as I sat down on my knees and looked into his eyes. He clenched his teeth and looked down at my hands on my lap.

"Yeah," he choked out. I shook my head.

"Jack," I whispered closing my eyes. "You need to tell someone about this. It's getting out of control!" I yelled. He shook his head.

"It's over now," he said coldly, acid in his voice.

"When did this happen?" I demanded. He leaned back, the marks on his arm really showing.

"Last night...he said something bad about you." He looked over at me, his eyes sweet but hard. "I hit him." A lump started in my throat. "We got into a fight. He hit me and I hit back just as hard." I didn't want to hear anymore. No. I had to let him finish. "He got me good in the stomach and I fell. He had the advantage and kicked me and kicked me...he was rough. Rougher than he had ever been. Finally, he gave up and yelled, screaming all this crap about respect." He scoffed. His voice sounded a lot better. Something of hope filled me a little. "Then this morning I couldn't get up for school. I was in pain. He got mad. He came in and hit me again till I finally left..." He looked back at me adjusting his jaw. "And here I am," he said. I didn't realize how I felt like hitting that man so hard he would die.

"Where's your mom?" I asked, my voice tense. He shook his head.

"She was at work this morning. Last night she yelled but she wasn't strong enough to stop him." I looked down. 'Calm down Lidia.' I told myself. 'It's okay.' I kept on having these visions of me killing him. It was horrible. Why did I care so much? I looked up at him.

"I'm glad you came," I said quietly as I reached for the wash cloth. I dipped it in the water and then looked at him again. His better eye was watching me; the light of the fire reflected sparkles of orange. I put my hand on his jaw and brought him closer to me. Even though he was badly bruised, he still looked handsome. Like those models that whatever you put on them, they still looked like sex symbols. I touched the wash cloth to his forehead where the wound was and he winced. "Sorry," I mumbled. I wiped off the blood. Well, it wasn't too bad. It looked like maybe he hit it on something when he fell. It already looked like it was healing. I looked down at his chest and bit the inside of my cheek so hard that I felt blood in my mouth.

"It doesn't hurt that much," he said, still looking at me. I avoided his eyes as I put the hot wash cloth on his bruised chest and shoulder. He flinched slightly as the hot water touched his cold body. I took it off and wiped his arm where the finger prints were; in an effort to make it feel better.

"Are your ribs OK?" I asked. I looked up at him. He moved a little bit and winced. Panic stirred in me.

"Yeah, I think...just muscles are sore." I nodded pressing my lips together.

"How are you feeling?" I asked. He shrugged a little.

"Better, but sleepy." I nodded.

"Okay, go to sleep."

"Lidia, please don't tell anyone. I'm fine," he said quietly. I nodded as I stood up and picked up the wash cloth and cup looking like it was dyed red. "Wait," he touched my hand. I turned toward him. "Thanks." I smiled sadly and nodded. I covered him up with a blanket and went out of the room and into the kitchen. I dumped the cup of water and threw the cloth over the dish pan. I leaned against the cupboards suddenly feeling like a leaf getting blown away by the wind. I slid down the side and sat down on my butt. My hands were shaking a little as I closed my eyes and tears streamed down between them. How could he not want someone to know? It would stop Scott from doing this! If I just called the cops and reported Scott, they would take him away for good. And Jane, why wasn't she doing anything? Because she thought she loved Scott? Her son was getting beaten to no ends by him and she didn't even care! I couldn't handle this. I couldn't handle seeing him hurt. Why? Because I cared about him. More than I ever knew.

Chapter 36

That night I checked on Jack to make sure he was okay and when he was fast asleep I went upstairs to my room, leaving my door wide open to hear if he needed me. I fell asleep.

The night was filled with nightmares. Every time I woke up, it would disappear but then, when I fell asleep again a new one would start. It always started with Jack getting hurt. And then it was me and then...him dying and me watching. It was horrible. But every time it was a different thing that killed us. The first time it was Scott. That was the worst one I had ever had. The second time, it was a tornado. The third time it was a zombie attack. I know it was weird and it was also a Dawn of the Dead moment but it scared me. I had to watch him get ripped apart. I woke up crying the last time. I remember it clearly. We were standing beside the big tree, laughing at something. Then in the distance we saw two people walking towards us. I frowned. It was Kendra and Grant. Kendra was wearing my white summer dress and Grant was wearing what Jack was wearing. I glanced over at Jack and he was frowning too.

"Ollie," Grant said his voice fading with the wind. It was strange and too sweet. "Come with me." He reached his hand out and I frowned, clearly wondering why they were doing this.

"Jack, come here," Kendra coed. We both walked forward and took their hands. Grant's were warm and hot as I placed my cold ones in his. They led us out into the middle of the field and turned us to face each other. I tried to speak but I couldn't. Jack and I stared at each other as Grant and Kendra circled around us. I looked behind Jack and saw Grant smiling wickedly. When I tried to move my feet, they wouldn't. Jack looked behind me and his eyes bulged into horror. He reached over and grabbed my hands and I held on as I knew what was coming. Grant lifted his knife above his head and I screamed but nothing came out as it raced toward Jack. At the moment it hit him, something also hit me, searing pain down my back. I woke up in a cold sweat, flinging myself up. I put my hand to my heart and tried to calm my breathing. I closed my eyes and exhaled. It was just a dream. It felt so real though. Kendra and Grant had stabbed us in the back. I looked at the clock and saw that it was only 8:00 a.m. I looked over and saw a little light coming through the cloudy sky but then it disappeared. I stood up and tip-toed to the window. Five inches of snow covered my car and the ground. I smiled. It was just lightly snowing now. I sighed and a cloud of breath formed on the window. Christmas Reindeer stood by in Mr. Roger's yard with a Santa on a sled. Christmas would be here in a week and a half. I'm glad Mom and Dad will actually be home this time. Last year they went to Australia and it didn't snow at all. They left me after we opened presents on Christmas morning. Actually we all went our separate ways, even though I wanted to spend Christmas with them. But they will be home for it this year. And we will spend it with each other. I pulled on a pair of jeans and a black woolen sweater. I went downstairs and saw Jack still sleeping with the curtains drawn across the window. I went over to him and looked at his forehead. It was healing quickly but I needed to get cream for it. I leaned over him and kissed his forehead softly. I put another cover on him and he groaned and turned on his side. I got my coat and wrapped myself up well before heading out. The '7 Eleven' was only about a block away and seeing that my car was covered in snow and probably wouldn't start, I decided to just walk.

When I got in there I grabbed a tube of cream for Jack, a box of doughnuts, a bottle of soda, and snacks of all sorts before paying for my shopping. I knew that if we got snowed in we would have to have food so I got everything I could. As I was getting closer to the house the wind picked up and snow started to pound down on me. I looked down, shaking as I pushed my feet towards the house. I unlocked the door quickly and ran in, shutting it. I sighed as I dropped the bags and peeled off my jacket, scarf and gloves. I kicked off my boots and went to the kitchen to put away the food. I sniffed, my nose stuffy.

"Where were you?" I turned around and saw Jack holding his side with a small smile on his lips. He had put his shirt back on.

"I had to get some things. Are you hungry? I got doughnuts." He grinned.

"I love doughnuts."

I laughed but felt like I shouldn't, since he still looked pretty bad. His black and blue eye looked better, but it was still swollen. He walked with a little limp as he went to the table where the doughnuts were. I grabbed the cream and went over to the table where Jack ate a doughnut. I scooped a bit with my finger tip then looked down at him.

"Look up," I said and he did. I looked into his eyes for a moment seeing that he could actually see with his black and blue eye. It was an intense gaze. There were no jokes or sarcastic comments, just a special one. One that explained how we were feeling. I looked away and put the cream on his cut and he winced a little. "How is your eye?" I asked quietly.

"OK, I think," he answered. I put the cap back on the cream. I went back over to the kitchen and put away the stuff then sat up on the counter and ate a granola bar. "I should probably call my mom," Jack said, standing up with a doughnut in his mouth. I nodded. "Maybe I should go home, too," he said with a frown. I frowned and stopped eating.

"Jack what I—."

"It's okay." He came over to me and put his hand on my knee, not really thinking. "It's just…I don't want him to hurt my mom." I looked away. "Hey," he said and rolled his eyes. He made me look at him. "Don't worry. Seriously, I'll be better in no time. It might be the worst I've gotten, but I'll survive."

"For now," I muttered. He clenched his teeth. "Jack if you don't tell the cops, I will," I told him. He was biting his tongue. I could tell.

"Lidia, you can't." I shook my head.

"Why the hell not?! You're being abused by your mom's boyfriend!" He put his doughnut down and I saw white powder on the edge of his mouth. I smiled lightly.

"What?" he asked angrily. I snorted.

"You have powder on your mouth."

"Oh," he said his voice softer. He wiped his mouth but it didn't come off. I laughed and he grew pink on the cheeks. I took a small towel from the sink and wiped the edge of his lip.

"There, got it." I smiled at him. He just laughed. He was closer to me now, standing in between my legs and I felt heat run through me. He didn't notice. I swallowed. I'm not sure how long I will be able to handle this. My hormones keep getting in the way of this fake relationship. I sighed and pressed my lips together.

"Listen, I'll call my mom and see how she is okay?" I nodded. He left the room and I took a deep breath. 'You like him,' my mind told me. 'You really like him.' I nodded. Yeah I do. I confirmed. Fireworks went off and cheering yelled in my head. I laughed a little. I jumped down off the counter and walked into the living room. I flinched as I remembered last night when he stumbled through the door. Jack was looking out the window talking on the phone. "OK, well just stay there...no I'm fine. You just stay at work until it passes...good you're with her...okay I'll call you tomorrow." His voice was soft and caring and I realized how he was sweet with his mom. More than any boy I'd ever met. He hung up and turned around to me. "My mom got stuck at work and is staying tonight till the snow is over," he said.

"Is she okay?" I asked. He nodded.

"Yeah, Scott hasn't been over." I nodded.

"Are you staying?" I asked quietly. He sighed and looked out the window at his car.

"Yup." He announced seeing his car piled up to the windows in snow. I laughed. "I think we're snowed in," he said and I laughed again.

"I'm glad we got food." He nodded. I stared a moment thinking of something special to me.

"There is this great place I know of. It's up around the mountains somewhere. My grandma used to take me there and we would stay for a week or two on holidays when my parents went away. It was always so beautiful in the winter," I said, deep in thought.

"You? No way! A country girl?" I looked at him and smirked.

"Sort of."

"What happened to your grandma?" I looked over at him and shrugged.

"She died a couple years ago and left the cabin to me." He raised an eyebrow.

"Sweet!" I laughed.

"Yeah, it's cool."

"Want to watch a movie?" he asked with a smile. I smiled back.

"Yeah."

I put the fire on and sat down on the sofa. Jack started a movie and sat close to me. I don't think he even noticed but I did. Our arms were touching. I wanted to hold his hand so bad. It was almost hurting me not to. 'Ignore it, Lidia.' OK. 'He doesn't like you that way.' I nodded to myself and watched the movie.

Chapter 37

We were halfway through the third Star Wars movie when Jack and I started to fight about it.

"Anakin deserved it!" I yelled.

"No, he doesn't! He was only doing it for Padmé. To save her." I shook my head and laughed.

"No, he shouldn't have listened to that jerk of a bad guy." Jack laughed.

"He didn't have a choice."

"Yes he did!"

Jack sighed.

"Can we please watch the movie?" he said, smiling. I rolled my eyes and stood up. It was almost pitch dark out and you could see that the snow had actually stopped. "Where are you going?" he demanded. I laughed.

"None of your business!" I said. He watched as I went into the kitchen. I got the hot chocolate from the cupboard and started to make two cups. "Do you want hot chocolate?" I yelled out.

"Yeah!" he said. I laughed. I put a cup of milk in the microwave and set it. Just as it was done, the lights flickered in the kitchen. I frowned.

"Shoot!" I muttered, and before I could get a flashlight the electricity went out. Everything was pitch black. I pushed myself against the counter hating the dark. "Jack?" I called. I heard him laugh.

"Coming."

I heard him scuffing his feet then I heard something hit the wall.

"Fu—!"

"Are you okay?" I asked. He chuckled.

"Yeah, I think." I heard him moving along the counter to the sink, then around to the bar. "Where are you?" he asked. I laughed knowing he was only a couple feet from me.

"Right here," I said and put my hands out. His hand smacked my arm.

"Oh! Sorry," he said. I laughed. I felt his shoulder and pulled him toward me. He laughed.

"Wow, so I wonder how long it's going to be out for," he mumbled. I shrugged.

"I have flashlights but we have to find them first."

He sighed dramatically.

"Great," I held his hand as I put my hand out and followed the wall. We had a shelf by the fridge that should have the flashlights in it. I could feel Jack close behind me; his breath tickling my ear. I reached my hand out to grab one of the flashlights but it fell with a thud.

"Crap," I muttered and got down on my knees.

"What're you doing?" Jack asked, laughing.

"I dropped the damn flashlight." Finally, my hands found it and I turned it on quickly. It flickered a little then became fine. I turned toward Jack who blinked and looked away. "OK, wow. Um, I have my old mp3 player in my purse in my room. That has the radio on it. We can listen and see if there are any power lines down." He nodded.

"Let's go, then." We turned and headed back to the den where the fire was just going out.

"Crap, we need to start that back up before it goes out."

"Let's get the radio first," he said. He held my hand as we walked up the stairs and into my room. I searched my purse until I found my mp3 player and got my ear phones.

"Got it!" I announced and turned back to him. He grinned.

"Good. Turn it on," I turned it on and put an ear phone in my ear. We walked slowly downstairs as I listened.

"It's on commercial." He laughed. Jack let go of my hand, went to stir up the fire and get it started again. I pushed the coffee table out of the way and placed the blankets and pillows on the ground like a bed and sat down. The fire blazed behind the grate and Jack wiped his brow and came and sat back down beside me. His arm touched mine and my heart rate spun out for a moment. I swallowed.

"Hear anything yet?" he asked. I realized I had been staring at him. The glow of the flames were making his skin look almost golden.

"Um, er, no, not yet."

He smiled and nodded. I started to listen, averting my gaze toward the black TV. It wasn't very bright in the den and I hated that.

"I think we need candles."

He nodded.

"Where are they?" he asked. I thought for a moment.

"In the drawer by the stove. Hold on, I'll help, but I want to listen." As I listened, the news reporter said that there was an accident down the road from us. A car had hit a pole. The people were okay, but the electricity was probably not going to come back till tomorrow or if not, in a day or two. I sighed and turned it off. "They said we probably won't get electricity back for a day or two."

He snorted.

"OK. Well, once my car gets uncovered we can go to my house or something." I nodded. We got the candles, lighted them and placed them around the room. The house smelled wonderful. With cinnamon and lavender and all sorts of scents. I looked at all the Christmas decorations and really thought it felt like Christmas. We sat back down again and I covered my legs with a blanket. "So are you sleeping down here tonight?" he asked, with a hint of a smile. I shrugged.

"I guess. I hate the dark." He laughed lightly.

"Afraid of the boogie monster?" I laughed.

"Yeah, a little."

"But I thought that Lidia Taylor wasn't scared of anything."

I thought for a moment.

"No...I am. I just hate showing it," I whispered. He looked at me and his blue eyes had that look in them. I could never quite comprehend the meaning of that look. He stared at me that way for a long time.

"When I think I know you…you just..surprise me," he said quietly, his voice distant but soft. I glanced over at him and hugged my knees to my chest. There were butterflies in my stomach that disrupted my thoughts.

"I thought that's what I was supposed to do. Surprise people." I looked over at him, amused. He smirked for a moment.

"You definitely do. But you're still mysterious." Those butterflies were making my mind go crazy. I looked over at him and looked away quickly. It took everything not to reach over and touch him. And I didn't know how long it would be until I gave up and did just that.

Chapter 38

"Are you going to college after high school?" I asked. He shrugged.

"I'm not sure yet. I don't know what I want to do. Maybe become a mechanic."

I nodded.

"A mechanic? Not bad."

He laughed a short and hard laugh.

"I'm not sure if I have enough money for college," he mumbled, staring down at the cup of water in his hands. I frowned.

"Couldn't you get a scholarship?" He sighed.

"You have to be very smart or athletic. And I'm neither." I made an 'O' with my mouth.

"That sucks."

"Tell me about it." It was silent for a moment. "So, you want to be a doctor?" I nodded.

"Always have. My mom…," I shook my head.

"What?" he asked.

"She doesn't want me to do anything like that. She wants a perfect Barbie doll daughter. And I'm nothing like that," I told him, my voice annoyed and angry.

"Yeah, I know that!" he muttered. I snorted and rolled my eyes. I nudged him playfully on the arm. He nudged back but kept his arm touching mine.

"No. it's just…she wants me to be fake. She thinks I can't get a guy if I don't let my boobs hang out and wear short skirts. She thinks men should take care of women. And let women shop and drown in their selfish little lives." I said angrily as my hands turned into fists. Jack was watching silently. "I hate it. I hate her sometimes. The way she doesn't say anything when she knows Dad cheated on her. I never ever want to be like her." I shook my head in disgust. "Either way, I'm going to college and becoming a doctor." I stared off into the fire, feeling its warmth.

"You should do what you want to," Jack said. "I think any woman should be able to do and say what she wants. Don't listen to your mom. She doesn't know." I looked at him and my stomach felt heavy. "And I know for a fact you will succeed in anything you try." His words sounded so different. They sounded kind and soft and truthful.

"You think I can do it?" I whispered. He smiled and nodded.

"I know you can." I smiled.

"And you? Do you believe in yourself?" He looked down. His black and blue eye was actually open but still a little sore.

"Not really. But I'll survive." He smiled halfheartedly. I frowned.

"Why?" I asked. He shrugged.

"My life is screwed up, Lidia. It's hard to keep your head held high when you have people telling you that you can't do anything." My heart was aching for him. I sat closer, leaning further toward him and keeping my eyes on him.

"Keep your head high even when people tell you that you can't. I think you can do anything and live through anything as long as you watch the prize ahead of you." He got closer, his eyes serious.

"And what would that prize be?" I bit my bottom lip feeling my breath getting faster.

"Whatever you want it to be." My body was craving him and I knew it was going to take over my mind. I wanted him so badly. The way he looked at me; the way he saw me. I can't just say I have no feelings. Oh I do! His eyes wanted something. It made me think thoughts and I wanted to make them come true.

"Jack," I whispered. He leaned forward and kissed me lightly but it made my head buzz. He pulled back and smiled sadly. I opened my eyes and swallowed. He looked at me and I stared back. His mouth was open slightly and all I could think was I wanted it back on mine. His eyes were so intense. Something in them told me that he was thinking the same thing I was. I sat up on my knees and put one on either side of him. His eyes didn't get wide or shocked. I leaned down and kissed him again as his hand wound around my waist. I pulled back, hair getting in his face. We looked at each other while my hands traveled down his chest then under his shirt. I brought it up and he put his arms up and threw it off. He slid his warm hands under my shirt and pulled it off of me. It fell to the floor. I kissed him again as he undid my bra, letting it fall to the ground. He put his warm hands on my back as I kissed him with my eyes tightly shut. He took hold of my legs, turned me over and laid me back on the blanket softly. Like he was messing with a delicate glass vase. He looked down at me and ran his hand down from my cheek to the middle of my breast to my belly button making a shiver run down my spine. My lower stomach throbbed for him. My body ached in places I wanted him to touch me, in ways that I had never felt before. He undid my jeans and slid them down. My normal breathing was hard to maintain. He let his hand slide down my thigh to my knee then back up. I watched him and saw that look of happiness and...something else...I put my hands to his pants and pulled them down slowly. He kicked them off. I put my hands on his neck and brought him down to me, kissing him again. My body was on fire from his body being so close to me. I felt the bulge from his boxers on my leg and I shivered again knowing what was going to happen and wanting it. He kissed down my neck to my chest where that freckle was and kissed all around my breast. I moaned quietly. I felt my lower stomach craving for more. He kissed down to my belly button and all around it. Down onto my hip then lower then on my thigh. I moaned louder grabbing his head. He came back up and kissed me with force. I gently pushed him over and got on top of him. I saw the bruise on his chest and kissed it. I kissed his neck then up to his lips. I kissed his eyelid softly then his forehead. I looked down at him and kissed his chest, his hip, his thigh where the bulge was getting bigger. I nipped at his tanned skin just close enough to the bulge. He groaned roughly. I came back up and pressed myself against him and he winced as I hurt his chest too much. I pulled back, my eyes wide.

"I'm sorry," I whispered. He smiled.

"It's fine." He pushed me back over and I took a deep breath. He put his hand down at my underwear and gently removed them. I felt self-conscious again as he looked down at me. Like I said, I wasn't the skinniest, but my curves weren't bad. He put his hand on my cheek and leaned down on me to kiss my neck. I put my hands in his hair and closed my eyes. He sucked softly and then he got to my spot. I gasped again and opened my legs up. He leaned close to me to let me feel him. I pulled him closer wanting it more now. He pulled back and pulled down his shorts. He flipped them off as I looked down at him. He blushed a little. I smiled and put his lips back to mine. I trailed my tongue along his and it wiggled to life. I moaned again. "Now?" he asked, between our lips. I nodded and braced myself. He pulled back and I felt him gently go in me. I gasped because it hurt. "Am I hurting you?" he asked, panic in his voice. He pulled himself back out.

"No, no, it's okay," I said, my breath catching. It felt good but it hurt. It felt strange but something in me said it was natural. He tried it again and it didn't hurt as much. As he went in again I felt myself getting hotter and hotter. He was groaning as he kissed my neck. I kissed him again and moaned as he went out and in. He was doing it slowly and sweetly as I held onto him and kissed him, everything feeling so good. He didn't want to hurt me and didn't want to do anything that would be uncomfortable. I could feel him getting closer and I was too. He sucked on my neck and I moaned louder than I had before. My fingernails dug into his back as we came together and I felt everything! My eyes could only see him and his blue eyes were staring down at me. I smelled his bittersweet cologne. My head was foggy, but I liked it. He groaned.

"Lidia," he said in my ear, his breathing heavy. I grabbed his hair, liking the way he said my name like that. In a desperate need. A sexual one. Begging almost.

"Jack," I whispered into his ear. A ripple went down his body and I arched my back wanting him the whole way in me. He moaned. I leaned up to him feeling sweat on both of us. "Faster," I whispered breathlessly in his ear. He admittedly did as I told and started thrusting into me faster. I steadied myself and took each thrust easily. I moaned, wanting to say his name but knowing I shouldn't. He started to thrust faster to where I was going to come again. I gave out a muffled cry as we both finally did. He was out of breath as he fell halfway down on me. Sweat beaded on his forehead as he looked down at me. It was another intent gaze. He pushed my hair back from my face silently. He pulled himself out of me and fell down beside me. I turned on my side to him and pulled a blanket off the floor onto me and onto him. He turned on his side, facing me.

"This was my first time," he said quietly. I raised an eyebrow.

"You haven't done it before?" I asked, surprised. He half smiled and shook his head. "I haven't either." We both looked at each other. We didn't touch again; we just stared into each other's eyes. We both settled down and I fell asleep, watching him looking golden and glorious by the fire blazing behind the grate.

Chapter 39

I felt a tickling on my palm. I frowned and my hand jumped. I heard a quiet laugh. It started again but somehow I liked the feel of the hard finger tips touching my hand. I opened my eyes and looked at Jack who was perched on his elbow, his hand tickling my palm lying open on the pillow beside my head. He had his jeans on but no shirt. His boxers were showing from under his pants. His hair was messy but he was still very cute. His chest still had the fading bruise on it and his eye was a little swollen. His blue eyes were a lighter color than usual but his lips were in a small smile. I smiled back and sighed.

"That tickles," I mumbled. He laughed again.

"I noticed," he said, using his husky, sweet voice. He stopped. I looked over at him.

"I like it." He stared at me with a smile still on his lips. I shivered as I remembered the previous night. The way he ran his fingers down my body... "What time is it?" I asked before he could say anything. He grabbed his cell phone from behind him and flipped it open.

"7:30 a.m." I yawned.

"Ugh, it's too early." The sunlight came in through the window and I pulled the blanket up around me. He chuckled.

"The electricity didn't come back but the fire went out sometime last night," he said. I nodded, closing my eyes again, feeling his fingers still on my palm. Last night...was amazing. It was probably the best night of my life. I care so much about him. More now than I did before. I could feel him close to me. If we did it, then maybe he liked me back. Just the thought of it made my heart jolt. But I wasn't going to say anything. Not yet. Maybe he'll tell me he likes me and we can actually be together for real. I smiled but then frowned. But doesn't he like Kendra? Wait, didn't I like Grant? What happened to our goal? I don't think I like Grant anymore. Does he still like Kendra? Is that why he slept with me? Because he wanted to brag to Kendra about 'doing it' with me? Jack pulled the cover back. I looked up at him as he smiled down at me.

"Thinking?" he asked. I nodded. "I can see the smoke," he joked. I didn't laugh or smile. He frowned. "What's wrong?" he asked coming closer to me. He pushed my hair behind my ear and I repressed myself from shivering from his touch.

"Nothing," I answered licking my chapped lips. He frowned even more. I closed my eyes again avoiding his eyes and sighed. I felt him lay down next to me and his hand was left by my hair. He curled his finger around the end then let it twirl back again. It felt good. The worry I had about him using me to get back at Kendra vanished. I don't even care if he used me or not! I was getting a lot out of it! He let his fingers run from the end of my hair past my collar bone to my back and made a single circle. Goose bumps appeared on my arms. He laughed a throaty laugh. I smiled.

"Mm, stop," I mumbled. He laughed again.

"Don't you like it?" he whispered, his voice joking and teasing. I nodded my eyes still closed. He didn't stop, hell I never wanted him to.

"I need to get up," I muttered, opening my eyes. He shrugged, taking his hand off me. I turned onto my back and rubbed my face, pushing back my messy hair. I probably looked horrible. Jack was quiet and I looked over at him, frowning. He was staring at my chest. My bare chest and stomach. I quickly grabbed the cover and covered myself up, blushing a little. He laughed and winked at me. I rolled my eyes. I sat up and made sure the blanket was around me tightly. I yawned again and stood up. Jack looked up at me with a small frown. "I think I'm going to get in the shower," I said, feeling sticky. He smirked.

"Want me to come, too?" I rolled my eyes again.

"No, thank you," I said, even though I wanted him to. He laughed.

"Fine, fine, fine. I'm going to get something to eat." He stood up and I went up the stairs, dragging the blanket with me. I got jeans and a T-shirt from my drawers, along with my innerwear. I went to the bathroom and stripped. As I looked at myself in the mirror, I realized how bad I looked. My hair was a rat's nest and my makeup was running. I looked tired but my skin was glowing, almost. I smiled and the girl in the mirror smiled, too. I turned on the shower and got in. I turned the knob so it was hot and let the water run over me. When I saw the blood going down into the drain, it hit me. Tears wheeled up in my eyes and I almost fell to the floor. I leaned against the wall, grabbing myself so the sobs wouldn't hurt so much. But they did. I cried hard. I realized that I wasn't a virgin anymore. I wasn't a little girl. My innocence was lost. And I had actually made a promise to stay a virgin until marriage. 'I can't believe I let this happen,' I thought, grabbing my hair. I didn't make the promise with my parents. They figured I'd do it so all they promised me was the pill! But I promised myself and my grandma that I would stay a virgin until my wedding night. I would show my parents that I could. I screwed it up! I cried harder. I screwed it all up. Like I always seem to. I stared at the shower curtain while the water ran, my eyes still full with salty tears. I couldn't believe I'd just had sex with Jack. I probably won't even marry him! Even if...even if I would, he would never want to be with me. I scoffed then sniffed. Okay, so I screwed up. I asked for forgiveness. I got it. I sniffed again and wiped my tears. I couldn't let that happen again. I went back to the water and let it drain everything away. I was not a little girl anymore and I would pay for this one day.

Chapter 40

After I cleaned myself up and got dressed, I could still feel the pressing weight of everything on me. I didn't want to tell my mom as she wouldn't understand. She would just say something like, 'Oh well, it had to happen sometime.' I wanted someone to say that it was okay and that maybe it was meant for after marriage but because things do happen, you can't really get punished for having sex before marriage. But I could definitely pay for that, because Jack didn't wear a condom. I know that for a fact! But right now I would gladly take anything that might happen, any sort of punishment, because I'd had sex before marriage. I tried to tell myself that it was okay. Doctors are always prompting it. Safe sex! It's okay! No. Sex was made for two people who both have a ring on their fingers and who have promised each other their hearts. I had to screw it up, didn't I? Now on my wedding night, I will be thinking about Jack. When my husband is kissing me, I will get a picture of Jack. How horrible is that? To try to have sex with your husband and get a picture of the guy you lost your virginity to? As I walked down the stairs, I tried on a fake smile but it didn't quite work. Jack was eating cereal and reading the newspaper. Suddenly, I stopped and stared at him. A vision flashed across my mind of him sitting there in a mechanic uniform with the words 'Walker' printed on his chest. His hair was the same but his jaw and body was older. He looked to be about 35. And the thing that stopped my breathing was the gold band around his wedding finger. Before I could really see anything more I blinked my eyes and the same old Jack was there.

"Lidia?" Jack asked, looking up at me. His blue eyes were cornered. How could I have seen him like that? It's not like we were going to get married! This was fake! This relationship had been fake! Why did it come to this?! Us sleeping together? Why?

"Nothing," I mumbled and walked quickly into the kitchen. I got a long drink of water. I felt a hand touch my hip and I flinched slightly. Jack put his bowl in the sink coming around me. "Sorry," he said and turned the water on, filling the bowl up.

"We have a dish washer, you know?" I said. He snorted.

"They don't work as good. And I'm just soaking it." I raised an eyebrow. He half-smiled.

"Never mind."

"So, your mom makes you wash the dishes, I'm guessing?" He laughed and blushed a little.

"Occasionally." I smiled. I turned and winced as my lower stomach was sore.

"Are you okay?" Jack asked, quickly turning towards me. I smiled sadly.

"I'm just...just a little sore." He looked down and then back up at me quickly.

"Um…oh," he said and turned around. I almost smirked but didn't. I got a bowl of cereal and ate it while Jack went back into the living room. After I was done, I went in too, and looked out the window. I heard the sofa squeak as Jack stood up. The snow was almost gone. It looked like a lot of it had melted from the sun that was shining brightly that morning.

"Wow," I muttered.

"Yeah, I should probably head home. I'm sure my mom is there now." I nodded and turned to my right to see him standing next to me holding part of the curtain up. His blue eyes looked light and bright. My heart beat speeded up again. He looked down at me and smiled. One of those breathtaking smiles. Before I could stop him, he leaned down and kissed me. He pulled back just as fast. I stared wide eyed at him. Why did he do that? That couldn't be fake! Maybe he does like me. "Let's clean up," he said. I nodded and we cleaned up the blankets and trash. As I put the blankets away, the lights flickered and came back on. "The lights are back on!" Jack yelled. I laughed.

"No, duh!" I shut the closet door and ran down stairs. Jack was switching the lights and the TV off.

"There, I think the house looks a little better," he said, looking around. I laughed.

"Good thing my parents won't be home till next week." He laughed along. "Um, I washed your jacket because...um there was blood on it. It's in the laundry." Jack nodded biting his lip. "I'll go get it, quick." I ran up the stairs and pulled out his brown leather jacket and smelled it. It smelled good. I went back down and Jack was putting on his shoes. "Um..." I said putting my hair behind my ear. "Here it is." I walked down the stairs and handed it to him. He looked at me and looked at it. He held it with his hand. But, I didn't let go. He wouldn't either. My stomach stirred as we stared at each other. Finally, I let go and he took it.

"Thanks," he said, sounding a little disappointed for a moment. I cleared my throat.

"How are your bruises?" I asked. He shrugged and touched his shoulder.

"OK, I think. Just still a little sore." He touched his forehead and winced. My heart ached. He laughed a little. "Yeah, just a little sore." I frowned but nodded. It was silent for a moment.

"Well...um I'll see you I guess sometime..." I said, not knowing what to say. He looked down and then back up at me. He looked a lot like a little puppy with his black and blue eye. But something serious stirred in them. He walked up to me and I looked down because I was on the step in front of him. He dropped his coat and my breath got heavy as he reached for me. I gladly took hold of him as he kissed me, wrapping his arms around my waist so tightly, though I wanted him closer. We both seemed to remember last night and his kisses grew rougher. I grabbed his hair in my hands and bit down onto his lip and he shivered slightly. He slipped my legs out from under me and laid me down onto the stairs. He got on top of me and pressed himself close. I moaned between our kisses. I spread my legs open automatically and he gladly got closer. As I felt him, I moaned harder and pulled away. He kissed my neck looking for that spot.

"Jack…," I said and he thought I was moaning it but I wasn't. "Jack." I said louder trying to sound more under control. He pulled back, his face flushed.

"What?" he asked.

"Your mom is going to wonder where you are," I said and took in a deep breath. He frowned and nodded. He stood up and straightened his shirt. I sat up, my lips feeling swollen. I tried to cool down my body. The thoughts of him using me to get back at Kendra and taking my virginity came to my mind and I clenched my teeth. He pulled his coat on and zipped it up. I looked at his face and suddenly I envisioned him smirking at me and saying "You are so easy. Just like the slut I knew you were. I lied to you about me not being a virgin, too. You're so gullible! Wow, Taylor. You are so stupid." A lump grew in my throat. He was. He was doing this to me on purpose. Leading me on, having sex with me, making me like him. It was all his plan.

"I'll call you tonight."

"No!" I said quickly looking up at him. He lifted an eyebrow his eyes confused. "No, that's not a good idea," I said, feeling anger in me. He frowned.

"Are you alright?" he asked.

"I'm fine! Why does everyone ask me that? If I wasn't fine, you would know!" I yelled suddenly. He flinched slightly.

"What the hell is your problem?" he asked. I growled.

"Nothing!" He glared.

"Whatever."

He turned his back to me. I ran down the steps, not finished with him yet.

"Actually I do have a problem!" I yelled. He stopped and I almost ran into him. He turned.

"Oh really?" he asked.

"Yeah! Your arrogance!" I said. He raised an eyebrow and laughed coldly.

"My arrogance? Well, then let's talk about you for a minute." I glared and crossed my arms. He looked at me, his eyes cold as ice. "You're stubborn and you won't listen to one damn thing! You don't care about anything but yourself just like all the sluts from school!" he yelled. My eyes got wide with anger. I lifted my fist and was about to pound his face in. He just smirked at my hand. "Go ahead. Do it," he said. I bit my tongue hard and I tasted blood. He put his face right at my fist and looked directly into my eyes. "Go ahead, Lidia. Free shot. I don't hit girls." I wanted to throw my fist at him so badly, but instead I withdrew it.

"Well, then I guess I can't hit you," I muttered coldly. He threw daggers at me with his blue eyes.

"Why are we even in this discussion?" he said, throwing his hands in the air.

"Because you're a jerk!" I yelled. He looked at me.

"If I'm a jerk, why are you still with me?" he shouted. We both looked taken aback by this. I grounded my teeth together.

"To get Grant back," I said quietly. He snorted.

"We both know it isn't working," he said through gritted teeth. I looked away, my hands still clenched in fists. "Why are you still with me, Lidia?" Jack asked quietly. I shook my head. Get a backbone Lidia! He's trying to get you to spill your guts and admit that you care for him. Once you say you care for him he's going to bend your words and use them against you. I snorted and looked up at him.

"For kicks, I guess." I gave a short laugh. Hurt showed in his eyes and I regretted saying it.

"Yeah, I guess so... I'm out of here," he said and flew open the front door and slammed it shut. After I heard the car tires squeal out of the driveway, my legs felt like jelly. I went to the steps and sat down. My head throbbed and I held onto it. Why did I just say those things? It's the opposite of what I wanted to say. How could I think those things about Jack? He wasn't like that! My mind took over me and I used my own words to hurt myself. I cried a little. I can't do this. I just have to tell him I care for him. Even if he laughs in my face.

Chapter 41

If only I knew that that day was going to be the worst day of my life. If only I knew that that call was going to make me almost die right there, I would have let the phone go. But I didn't. That's the thing. You don't know what's going to happen and you can't regret what does.

10:34 a.m.

I decided then that I was going to call Jack. I couldn't let what happened last night wreck our fake (or not) relationship. I picked up the phone by my bed and dialed his number. I frowned as it went straight to voice mail. I did it again. Same result. I frowned. He never had his phone off. I called for the 10th time. No answer. I stopped and decided I would call my parents. It rang 4 times and then dad picked up. "Hey bud!" he said, cheerfully.

"Dad, hey. How is everything going?" I asked, hopeful. He laughed, sounding a little nervous. "Pretty good."

"Ooh! Let me talk to her!" I heard in the background. It was Mom.

"Okay, here," Dad said.

"Hey, baby!" Mom said, all happy.

"Hey. Are you guys okay?" I asked. Mom giggled.

"Yeah we're fine! Actually, we're great!" This surprised me.

"So, it's working?" She giggled again and said something to my dad.

"Yes, it is. So how is everything there with you?" I sighed. I wanted to gush my heart out to her and I was about to when I heard her saying something to my dad after which she giggled. "Oh, Mark, stop it! I'm talking to our daughter!" I gagged mentally. "Sorry, honey. What is it?" I knew they weren't stopping.

"Mom, it's just...I think I really lo—"

"Mark! Don't tickle me!" she screeched into the phone. I clenched my teeth. "Honey, how about I call you back in about-" Giggle. "--- 20 minutes? Your father---" Giggle. "--- is being a butt!" I was just pissed at this point.

"Whatever." I turned off the phone and threw it across my bed. I curled my legs to my chest and put my chin on my knees. Tears formed in my eyes. My mother won't even talk to me. I have no friends. I could call Candice, but she wouldn't understand. I bit my lip and stared at the wall with a boy band poster on it. What did I get myself into? I'm tangled in a web. I'm the fly in the web struggling to get away while two big spiders are making their way across the web to kill me. To string me up and feed me to their young. I jumped as my phone vibrated. I rolled my eyes. 'Probably Mom saying she was done screwing my father!' I thought sarcastically. I picked up the phone and looked at the number. I frowned as I didn't recognize it. I picked it up, anyhow. "Hello?" I asked.

"Lidia!" Jane said, her voice sobbing. "Lidia, Jack...Jack...he's in the hospital." At that moment, every sound and nerve in my body froze. My mind went completely blank. But then I saw a vision of him. His eyes smiling. That strange smile that I couldn't figure out the meaning of. Then everything came rushing back like a giant wave.

"What?" I asked breathless. She sobbed.

"He got into a fight with Scott...and...and they started to fight. Jack...he got hurt very badly and he's in the hospital." I swallowed hard. "Jack! He's hurt, Lidia! You need to come now!"

"Where?" I demanded. Anger rushed in me just as quickly and I wanted to murder Scott.

"The main one. I'm here now."

"I'm coming," I said, hanging up.

Chapter 42

"Can you tell me where Jack Walker is please?" I begged the lady at the reception. A thousand things raced through my mind as I drove to the hospital. Was Jack dying? Was he in a coma? Will I ever be able to talk to him again? Oh god...the things I said when we fought! How could I have done that? The lady took a double take when she saw how tense and wired I was.

"Oh...yes. Room 225." I ran down the hall and searched. Finally, I came to a halt at the door. His door. Jack's hospital door. Before I could go in, it opened. I jumped as a nurse came out, holding a needle. My blood grew cold.

"Hello," she said sweetly and then moved around me. Jane sat in a chair by his bed holding his hands. Before I knew it, I was hyperventilating as I looked at Jack. He was bruised, his swollen eye looked better but I could see the giant bruises on his arms. His shoulder and arm were in a cast. His knuckles were a little bloody and scabs on them. His eyes were closed in a peaceful state but his lip and eyebrow were cut again.

"Lidia!" Jane breathed as she looked up at me. Her eyes were red rimmed, her makeup was smearing down her cheeks. Her hands were shaking a little as she wiped the tears away. She stood up and came over to me. I couldn't breathe. My eyes wouldn't leave the boy in the hospital bed. Jack Walker, my fake relationship boyfriend. My Jack. Yes, I claim him. Jane hugged me tightly and I didn't realize how tightly I was squeezing her until she let me go.

"How is he?" I asked, my voice shaking. She sighed and dabbed her eyes.

"The doctors say that he's okay. He broke a rib and his arm. The rest are bruises and scrapes. Other than that, he's okay." I nodded, relief filling my gut. But then guilt took over like a massive truck had hit me square in the stomach.

"What happened?" I asked. She took my hand, pulled me in and shut the door. She sighed and put her hand on her forehead.

"Jack got home late yesterday...Scott didn't care. I was just worried and was happy that he was home. But when I asked him where he was, he said nowhere. And then Scott said...," she paused and looked at me. "Scott said probably with his slut of a girlfriend and...Jack cracked. He grabbed Scott and I thought he was going to kill him. Lidia, I know my son. I'd never, ever seen that side of him before. I was frightened. Then Scott got really rough. I was screaming my head off at them to stop but they wouldn't. When Jack got hit and fell to the ground, that's when I called 911. They came and Scott had threatened me not to tell them what he did or he'd kill me..." She cried a little looking at me. "I couldn't take it anymore. I told the police what Scott had been doing for the past months. They took him to jail." She broke into sobs that racked her body. I hugged her again and almost smiled with relief. He was gone! God, he was finally gone! Jack was free!

"Jane, you did the right thing. He was hurting Jack!" I said. She nodded and sniffed.

"I know I did." She pulled back and wiped her eyes again. She looked back at Jack. "He's asleep now. But I'll give you some privacy." Suddenly I didn't want to be alone without her. I didn't want her to leave me alone with Jack. She straightened her shirt and smiled sadly at me. "I'm going to get a cup of coffee," she said and sniffed before she left the room. She shut the door and I heard it click shut as if a bomb was going off. I flinched. I looked at Jack again and realized something. He lying in the hospital bed was my fault. I choked as I knew it was the honest truth. If he hadn't come over, if he hadn't spent the night...if we hadn't gotten together, he would be safe at home. Scott wouldn't have hurt him. Scott wouldn't have said anything about me and Jack would be okay. But no, I had to say yes to his stupid plan and go along with everything! I yelled at myself mentally. I was flinching every second I yelled at myself for being an idiot. Before I knew it, I heard someone say my name. I blinked and looked. Jack was sitting up a little, his blue eyes open and staring at me. My mouth was agape.

"Lidia?" he asked. Tears spilled out of my eyes before I could control myself.

"Jack!" I ran towards him, my legs feeling like jelly. I wasn't sure if I could have made it to the bed but I did. He sat up and I wrapped my arms around him and he squeezed me tightly to him. "Jack...I'm—I'm so sorry! This is all my fault!" I choked on my tears. He winced a little as I hugged too tight, but I didn't care. Then his jaw clenched.

"It's not your fault. And it's okay," he said. I shook my head and pulled back and looked at him. Big drops of salty water fell from my eyes. His face looked sweet and sad all at the same time.

"Jack...I care for you...I really do," I took his better hand in mine and brought it up to my face. I pressed his palm on my cheek and closed my eyes tightly. His tough finger tips made my skin tingle and all I knew was that I really liked him. Maybe even more than that. He sighed and rubbed his thumb over my lips.

"You do?" he asked. I opened my eyes and looked at him.

"Yes," I finally admitted. He smiled but his eyebrows were together because it must have hurt.

"So, you want to do this?" he asked looking into my eyes. I frowned.

"Do what?" I asked. He smiled and that same incomprehensive expression showed in his eyes. Then I got what he meant. He meant our relationship. To make it real. I smiled and laughed a little. "Yeah." He put his hand in my hair and felt it. He looked at it as if it might disappear any minute. I felt my body tingle from his touch again. I felt relaxed that he was near. That I was with him. I felt good but still I could feel myself hurt every time I looked at him. I leaned down and kissed his forehead softly. When I pulled back, his eyes were closed. "How's your arm?" I whispered. He opened his eyes and shrugged.

"It's OK, I guess. Just a broken arm. Nothing new." I frowned. He lay back in the bed and looked up at me. Just staring. Finally he said, "My mom told you what happened, didn't she?" I pressed my lips together and pulled his hand down from my face and put it between my hands. I nodded. He didn't say anything.

"He's in jail," I said. I looked up to see his eyes wide.

"What?" he asked.

"Your mom told the police what happened and they put him in jail." He was still stunned. And I let him ponder as it sunk in.

"He's not coming back?" he asked. I shook my head with a smile.

"No, you're safe. Your mom and you are safe." His eyes looked like a ton of weight had been lifted off and I smiled brighter.

"Oh God...he's finally gone," he said, shaking his head. I patted his hand in mine and then my smile faded.

"You're in here because of me," I whispered. He suddenly looked at me, frowning.

"No, I did this to myself." I looked down. No, he didn't. "Hey," he tapped my chin so I would look up. His eyes were soft but hard and serious. "It's not your fault. Don't you ever think it was your fault," he demanded. I clenched my teeth but nodded. He sighed. "Where's my mom?" he asked as he pulled me down onto the bed with him.

"Getting a cup of coffee," I sniffed and laid my head onto his pillow and looked up at him. He put his arm around me. I felt safe. This, this felt right. How it was supposed to be. We were together now. Not officially, officially, but basically. Screw Grant! I didn't want him anymore. I didn't care about him anymore. I had Jack. Jack leaned down and kissed me softly on the lips and it was everything I wanted at that moment.

Chapter 43

I stayed late that night, just talking to Jack and his mom until the nurse kicked me out. Then I went home and called my mom.

"Yeah?" she asked in her perky voice.

"Um, Mom, Jack got hurt and he's in the hospital." Mom gasped.

"What?" she asked.

"He got into a fight with his mom's boyfriend and he got hurt badly. I went in and saw him today." She gasped again.

"Oh, that's horrible!" I bit my lip.

"Yeah, I was really worried about him. I mean he could have really gotten—"

"Hey, honey I have to go. The doctor here is starting the meeting. I'll call you when we're done." I stared blankly at the wall in front of me. "Honey?" she asked. "OK, I love you. Bye," she hung up as I just stared. My own mother doesn't even care. She doesn't care that my boyfriend could have died. I pulled the phone from my ear and turned it off. At that point I had lost all respect for my mother. I went to bed shortly after and cried a little as I fell asleep. But just remembering his smiling eyes helped me. I smiled softly.

The next morning, I took a shower and got into some warm clothes before grabbing Lord of the Flies and heading out. Except this time, I didn't go to school. I went to the hospital. The lady at the front desk smiled as I headed to Jack's room. I knocked before entering and caught Jack with a spoonful of soup going into his mouth. I smiled and shut the door.

"Your mom's not here?" I asked heading over to the chair beside his bed.

"Nope, she had work. And don't you have school?" I peeled off my jacket and scarf grinning at him.

"Playing ditchie." He raised an eyebrow grinning.

"I've taught you well," he said. I laughed and sat down, pulling my long sleeves around my hands to keep them warm. His room was cold.

"Yeah, that you have."

He ate his soup and then looked at me.

"You really should be at school," he said. I rolled my eyes.

"And why would you care if I skipped school? You did it a million times!"

"I didn't do it a million times!" he said, rolling his eyes. I raised an eyebrow. He sighed. "Just a..a lot."

"My point exactly." I sat down beside him. He put his arm around me and I leaned on his shoulder. "How's the food?" I asked.

"Like shit." I laughed.

"It's a hospital. I'll bring you something when I come next time." He nodded. I looked at his arm resting on my arm. It had a white tag on it showing his name. His rough fingers lightly grazed my arm up and down. I smiled. The small TV was on in the corner but when I looked at Jack he was staring down at our feet. "What's wrong?" I asked. He sighed.

"Nothing, just thinking." He looked at me and smiled tiredly.

"Are you sleepy?" I asked. He shrugged.

"A little." I put my hand on his cheek and it prickled from the tiny hairs on it.

"Go to sleep." I leaned up and kissed him lightly. But as I pulled away he pulled me back and continued to kiss me. His kisses were soft and sweet but as I got lost in it, I didn't realize that I was on top of him. He used his good arm to pull me closer, rubbing our hips together. I moaned. I put my hands around his neck and ran my hand through his hair. Someone cleared their throat and I jumped and looked toward the door. A nurse stood there, smirking at us.

"Mr. Jack needs to take his meds," she said. I got off of Jack and he sat up quickly, looking pink in the cheeks. She watched as Jack swallowed his pills. "Now, these will make you sleepy," she warned. She smiled at me. "Sorry. Have a nice day." She left and shut the door. I looked at Jack and he laughed. I did the same and slapped my hand to my face.

"You need to sleep," I said.

"Well, I kind of want to do something else," he said, winking at me.

I rolled my eyes. "We're in a hospital and you have a broken arm. I don't think so."

He grinned at me. "What I want to do doesn't have to involve hands..." My mouth dropped and he laughed.

"Go to sleep!" I yelled, blushing. He smiled and settled back on the bed to take a nap.

"Wake me up before you leave," he whispered.

"OK," I said, but I knew I wasn't going to. I hugged my knees as I looked around the room.

"I can't fall asleep," Jack said, opening his eyes. I sighed.

"Want me to read to you?" I asked. He looked over at me.

"Yeah," he said. I got my book out and showed him the cover. He grinned. I started to read and he laid back and closed his eyes, a strand of his hair falling into his eyes. Ten minutes later, I stopped and looked at him. His breathing was slow and soft. I smiled.

I felt something rough rub against my cheek and looked behind me. Jack's leather jacket! I pulled it off the side of the chair and down into my fingers. I smiled. I pulled it up and smelled it. It smelled like my detergent and him. I stood up and put my arms into the sleeves of the jacket and pulled my hair out from the back. It was big, but it was warm. I smiled as I quietly went out of the room to get a coffee from the cafeteria.

When I got back, I settled down in the chair and started to read to myself while sipping my coffee, enjoying Jack being this close to me.

Chapter 44

I looked up when I heard the bed squeak and Jack sighed and looked over at me.

"Hey, sleepyhead," I said quietly. He smiled and closed his eyes a little.

"What are you doing?" he asked. I picked up my book.

"Reading." He nodded and opened his eyes.

"Why are you wearing my jacket?" he asked. I blushed a little.

"I was cold," I shrugged. He beamed.

"It looks good on you." I rolled my eyes at him.

"Oh, good. You're awake." We both looked toward the door and Jane walked in, snow on her hat and a bag at her side.

"Oh, hello, Lidia!" She smiled at me.

"Hey." I put my book away and stood up.

"Here, I brought you some clothes from home." Jane said pulling out sweat pants and a T-shirt for Jack.

"Thanks mom," Jack said sitting up.

"Oh, shoot! I forgot your socks. They're in the car. Be right back!" She rushed out and I laughed.

"Hey, I think I'm going to head out," I said, starting to take off his jacket. He frowned.

"You don't have to," he said. I smiled.

"Yeah I do. I still didn't finish my homework." He laughed. I pulled off the jacket.

"Why don't you keep it for me?" Jack said. I looked at him.

"What?" I asked. He smiled.

"My jacket. Why don't you keep it so it doesn't get pitched here?" I was shocked. He loves this jacket and he's letting me take it?

"Are you sure?" I asked. He nodded, so sure of himself. "Okay." I pulled it back on and felt like I was wrapped in his arms. Though it had a slight smell of blood on it. "Um, thanks." I said. He nodded. I put on my scarf and gloves and went around the bed to him.

"I'll come back tomorrow." He smiled as I leaned down and kissed his cheek. I looked into his eyes, then gently kissed his lips. He sat still, savoring the kiss. I smiled and waved.

"See you tomorrow!" He nodded and smiled back as I left.

****

Three days later

School was out for the holidays so I didn't have to worry about going to the hospital. I happily went to see Jack every day and stayed till 6:00 p.m. or 7:00 p.m. He slept most of the time and when he wasn't asleep, I would read to him or we would just talk or laugh. We fought like two times about something extremely stupid. But we always got over it. I sat in the familiar chair and watched an old episode of 'House' with him.

"Dude, this guy is a jerk," Jack said pointing to the TV. I rolled my eyes. His arm was out of the cast but still in an Ace Wrap and he couldn't move it that much. Apparently it wasn't a break, just a really bad sprain. His bruises were healing nicely.

"He's not!" I said. He looked at me his hair messy and falling to the side more, raising an eyebrow. "Okay! So he is, a little bit," I admitted. He smirked. He was wearing a dark blue T-shirt and plaid sweat pants. "But come on! He's hot for a 40-year old!" He laughed and shook his head.

"You need to get out more," he said. I frowned.

"What do you mean?" I asked. He sighed.

"You're in here every day with me. It's Saturday. Go out and have fun or something." I rolled my eyes.

"What if I don't want to have fun?" He raised an eyebrow.

"You do. And once I get out of here we are going to have some fun." He winked at me. I laughed.

"And what makes you think I want to have fun with you?" He frowned.

"Well, I guess you'll lose out, then." I laughed again.

"OK, whatever. I have to run to the store now for some food."

I stood up and got my things together, placing Jack's leather jacket around me. I had worn it all week. I smiled as I walked out. He waved. I got out into the city and sighed as I went to the local market. Mom and Dad would be home today. They were getting out early because they didn't need the counselling anymore. They were OK. 'Surprise, surprise,' I thought coldly. I went into the store and grabbed some frozen pizzas, a small ready-made salad and a Gatorade. Just as I was about to go out the door, I ran into someone.

"Oh! Sorry," I muttered and looked up, pushing a piece of hair out of my face. It was Grant.

"Lidia! Wow, hey," he said, surprised just as much as I was. He actually looked really nice. He had his black ski jacket on with a matching hat and gloves. His blonde hair was coming out from the hat. This is how I remembered Grant. The sweet and charming guy.

"Um, hey. How are you?" I asked politely. He smiled and showed those white teeth.

"Good, pretty good. My dad just got promoted in his job." I raised an eyebrow.

"Wow! That's awesome. He's been trying to hit that for a while now, hasn't he?" He nodded.

"Yeah, he's real excited about it. So how are you?" he asked, quietly looking into my eyes. My breath almost caught.

"Um, good. Just hanging out, you know. Jack's been in the hospital, so I've been going in every day." Grant knitted his brows and nodded.

"I heard about that. Heard he got into a fist fight with his step dad or something?"

"His mom's boyfriend. Well now, ex-boyfriend. So I've been a little tied up." He nodded sympathetically.

"Well, actually there's a Christmas party at Jonathan's house tomorrow if you want to go." I smiled.

"That would be nice. Jack was trying to get me out of there anyhow." The look when I said Jack's name sparked a glare just barely visible in Grant's eyes but I knew him too well not to see it.

"Cool, then I'll see you there I guess." I nodded.

"Bye." We went around each other and I went to my car feeling unsure if I should really go to the party without Jack. Mm, I'll ask Jack tomorrow if I should.

****

When I got home, Dad and Mom were unpacking their stuff.

"Oh, hey, honey!" Mom said, rushing over to me to give me a hug. I hugged back a little. I was still upset with them.

"How's Jack?" she asked rubbing my arms. I shrugged.

"He's fine." She frowned.

"We should go in sometime to see him, Ian." Mom said, turning to dad. He shrugged, looking the same.

"Hi dad," I muttered. He nodded and gave me a quick hug. I put the food in the fridge as I heard Mom and Dad talking. Well, Mom was mostly giggling. Parents! I went up to my room quickly and shut my door. The school had given me extra work to do over the holidays so we wouldn't forget what we were doing. How fun is that? I started on the book they gave me and settled back in bed with a notebook by my side.

I guess I fell asleep, because the next thing I knew, I was dreaming. It was just flashes but it was more of a nightmare. Grant plunging a knife into Jack's back; the look of excitement on Grant's face; the look of pain on Jack's face...it hurt me. Then, I could feel Kendra behind me; I could see her face; she had the same look as Grant's; her eyes were blazing with fire. Then everything was gone but Grant and I. He was wearing his ski jacket and his matching gloves and hat. I stared at him, his eyes were kind, like they always were. He was smiling at me.

"I really miss you, Lidia. I want to be friends, maybe more if we can." He said sweetly. My heart melted. Was I falling back in love with Grant? No, I couldn't be! But this thing with Jack...it was fake. We might have had sex but does he really feel like that for me? Grant took my hands, brought them up to his heart and placed them there. I took a deep breath. "Lidia..." He moaned, closing his eyes. "Lidia," he said again but his voice sounded like a girl's. I frowned...

I sat up quick and pressed my lips together.

"Lidia?" Mom knocked on my door.

"Com—" I cleared my throat because it sounded hoarse. "Um, come in." Mom came in and smiled at me, her blonde hair up in a bun.

"Oh, I'm sorry honey. Were you asleep?" I rubbed my eyes and sighed.

"No. What do you need?" She came in smiling brightly.

"I just wanted to talk. We haven't seen each other for a week. And I want to know how Jack is." She put her hand on my knee. "And you," she said seriously. I felt my wall break down and I almost gasped when I felt tears in my eyes.

"Jack's hurt, Mom," I said simply. "But Mom, I'm so confused." She listened. Should I tell her? No, I can't tell her about the fake relationship between Jack and me. It's too hard to explain. I inhaled and looked at her. "Mom, I really like Jack but...I think I might still have feelings for Grant. What should I do?" I begged. Mom sighed and looked at me with sad eyes.

"Honey, I've never been in this kind of a situation before. But what I can tell you is, follow your heart." I raised an eyebrow. Mom laughed. "I know, I know. It sounds corny, but really honey, that's what you should do. Just do what your heart is telling you. That's all I can say." I frowned and looked down at my hands. What if my heart was as confused as I was? Something pounded a name in my heart, it bled the name, but I couldn't get hurt. Not again. I pressed my lips together and nodded.

"Thanks, Mom." She grinned.

"No problem, sweetie!" She paused for a minute and then giggled.

"Your father and I have been getting along great!" she said, thrilled with excitement. I really didn't want to listen, but I had to. She told me about her and Dad's experience with the therapist and how she worked wonders! I could care less. I thought of Jack in the hospital and decided I would go in first thing in the morning. I sighed. "So, now our sex life is great!" I stared up at her with wide eyes.

"Mom! Ewe! Stop it! I don't want to hear about that!" Mom laughed and patted my knee.

"I know, sweetie. Oh, well, I have work in the morning since they called in. Night." She kissed my head and left the room. I fell back in bed with tears stinging my eyes once again. My phone vibrated on my night stand and I reached out glumly and picked it up.

"Hello?" I asked.

"Lidia, are you OK?" Candice asked, sounding worried. I sniffed, clearing my voice.

"Um, no, sorry. What's up?" Candice was quiet for a second.

"OK...Oh! Um, I just found out that Kendra and Grant broke up last night." I raised an eyebrow.

"Really?"

"Yeah, Tommy said he and his friends were walking to the pizza place and Kendra stormed out crying. They asked some people and they said Kendra and Grant got into a huge fight in front of everyone at the restaurant." Wow, I never thought that would've happened. Even though Kendra and I weren't talking, maybe I should call her? She might need a friend.

"Is she OK?" I asked. Candice snorted.

"She's probably sleeping with a guy right now getting over--- Oh! Lidia, I'm sorry, I forgot you and her—"

"No, no, its fine. I know what people thought about her," I said calmly.

"Oh...OK, well I'm sure she's fine but, who knows. Listen I got to go. Tommy and I are going out. Just thought I'd let you know. Oh! How's Jack? Tommy and I went to see him yesterday but we didn't see you." She rambled on and I couldn't help but smile.

"Yeah, I was gone by then. OK, go, have fun. I'll call you tomorrow or something." Candice laughed.

"OK, bye!"

I hung up and sat my cell phone down. I curled into a ball and thought of calling Kendra.

Chapter 45

The next morning, I got up, took a shower and changed. I grabbed a candy bar and a pop-tart from the cupboard and headed to the hospital. I hugged Jack's jacket to me, trying to find that smell again. When I got to the hospital, Jack was awake and flipping through channels on the TV. He grinned when he saw me.

"Hey, Princess!" he said. I rolled my eyes but smiled. I kissed his cheek.

"Brought you something," I said, wiggling an eyebrow as I ate the rest of my pop-tart.

"Oh, yeah? What?" he asked. I pulled out the candy bar. He grinned even wider.

"Thank god! Real food! The food in this place sucks!" I laughed.

"Didn't Jane bring you anything?" I asked. He shook his head.

"Only some...stupid healthy stuff." I laughed again.

"She's your mother. You have to listen to her." He scrunched up his face. I laughed and shook my head. "Glad you're back," I said and leaned over to give him a kiss on the cheek. He moved instead and our lips met. He pulled me onto the bed and I could feel the lust and passion in his kiss. I was so surprised. I latched my hands in his hair as he bit down on my bottom lip. I moaned. I didn't hear the heart rate monitor till it was beating so loudly, that I pulled away quickly. Jack was panting and he looked at me. I smiled.

"Your heart would've beat out of your chest if we didn't stop." He laughed with pink tinted cheeks. I just smiled. But then I thought of Grant. He would never have blushed. Not for me at least.

Why was I thinking of him though? "I think we should stop for now." I said, pulling myself free of Jack. He frowned slightly. I sat back in the chair, calmed my breathing, and tried to regain my composure. "Um, so Jonathan Merith is having a Christmas party tonight. I was invited." Jack raised an eyebrow. I waited for him to say something.

"Are you going?" he asked. I shrugged.

"I'm not sure. I was waiting to talk to you first." He laughed.

"Lidia, why do you have to talk to me first? I'm not your father; you don't need to ask for permission."

"I wasn't going to ask for permission!" I said. "I was just going to see if you didn't care-"

"I don't. You need to get out for a while, anyhow. I mean, you've been in here every day with me. Get out, have some fun." I frowned.

"Are you sure?" He smiled.

"I'm positive." I smiled.

"Thanks." He laughed.

"You make your own choices Lidia. You're a big girl."

I watched him for a moment. Watching his red lips move, then his blue eyes shining at me. He was wearing old sweat pants with paint on them and a black T-shirt which was making his eyes look extra blue. There was a fluttering in my stomach.

"Okay, I'll go tonight," I confirmed. He nodded. But wait, Grant was going to be there. And, he and Kendra weren't together. I wouldn't know what to do if he talked to me. Maybe just go with it? The thought of seeing Grant actually made my heart rate bounce a second. Wait no! I thought I was over him?

"Something wrong?" I blinked and looked up.

"No, nothing's wrong, Jack," I said quietly. He still looked at me with an I'm-not-buying-it look. I can't tell him Grant is going to be there. Or that he broke up with Kendra. He would never let me go. Or maybe he would. But I thought I needed to talk to Grant. One last time. To really see how my feelings are towards him. I just hoped nothing was going to happen.

I left the hospital early to go get ready for the party at 6:00 p.m. Mom and dad were in the living room and I could hear the TV on and them talking. I stopped in and said hi.

"Oh, you're back early," Mom said. I nodded.

"I'm going to a Christmas party tonight." She raised an eyebrow.

"Without Jack?" I shrugged.

"Why?" I asked. She just shrugged, too. 'Witch of a woman,' I thought.

"I don't know. Is Grant going to be there?" She thinks I'm going to cheat on Jack!

"Um, I don't think so." I said, thinking it wasn't any of her business.

"Oh, OK. Well, have fun!"

I nodded and went up the stairs. My mom knew me. Maybe that's why she said that. But I wasn't going to do anything with Grant! I just wanted to talk to him. Is that called cheating? I looked through my closet and found some old clothes that I hadn't worn in a while. I found a black skirt. A little tight, though. A red silk shirt with a black vest. It was very punk. Maybe too punk, I thought. I used to be like that. Wear those clothes with my baggy pants. I had my own style. I didn't really go along with the flow. I was more of a stand-out person and I loved being that way. I knew girls at school talked about my clothes, but I really didn't care. I liked being different and standing out in a crowd. Now, I guess I was one of those girls. I slipped on a pair of boots, grabbed my jacket and headed back out to the jeep. "Bye," I called as I left. I was nervous as I started up the car. I swallowed and drove over to Jonathan's.

The house was rocking with music. There was all sorts of music, from rock, rap to Christmas music. I laughed as I heard someone shouting 12 Days of Christmas. He was obviously drunk. I knocked on the door and a girl opened it, dressed up as a slutty Santa drinking from a cup. She grinned when she saw me.

"Hey!" she yelled over the music. I didn't really know her but saw her around at school. "Come on in!" I went in and sighed as I saw people dancing and making out. Not exactly a Christmas party. "How are you, Lidia?" the girl asked. Oh, man. What was her name?!

"I'm good, you?" I called over the music. She laughed.

"I'm great! Want some beer? There's some in the kitchen." I shrugged.

"Maybe later."

She nodded and drank the rest of her beer.

"So, are you and Grant getting back together?" she asked. I looked over at her sharply.

"No! Why would you think that?" I asked bitterly. She was too drunk to hear my tone though.

"Oh, cause him and Kendra broke up and he was talking about you." Grant was talking about me?

"About what?" The girl burped loudly. I grimaced.

"About getting back together with you." I frowned.

"I don't know," I said quietly.

She cheered as someone jumped off the stairs and fell face first onto the carpet. Grant wants me back. For real! Not in a dream but for real.

"Is he here yet?" I asked. She cheered again before answering me.

"Yeah I think he's in the dining room or something. Go baby!" she yelled and ran towards a guy and started to kiss him. I took off my coat and placed it behind the steps. I didn't want any bozos trying to steal it or puke on it. I walked into the kitchen, dodging a guy who was running out, holding a keg. I grabbed a Coke out of the cooler. It was a lot quieter by the kitchen apart from an occasional shout or cheer. The kitchen branched off into the dining room and there I saw Grant. My breath caught for a moment. He was wearing nice jeans and one of those stupid brand-name shirts with the logo on the front. He had a beer in his hands and was talking to two other guys, one with a girl on his side. Seriously! She was basically clinging to him. The other guy was big and broad. Very scary looking, but I recognized him from the football team. I walked over and smiled.

"Hey," I said. Grant grinned at me. It was a little sloppy but still Grant.

"Hey Ollie!" He looked me down, then up and so did the other guys. The girl glared at me. She was wearing a short, short red skirt and a black knit top that was very low in the front. I just ignored her.

"So, what've you been up to?" I asked. The other guys and girl started their own conversation.

"Good! Great! I've been great. You know Kendra and I broke up right?" I laughed and nodded.

"Yeah, Candice told me." He nodded, not seeming bothered by it.

"What about you?" he asked me. I shrugged.

"Same, same. Just going to the hospital to see Jack." He ignored that.

"Want to go upstairs and talk?" he asked out of the blue. I stuttered and then finally said, "Sure." That wasn't what I wanted to do but hey, I did want to talk to him, right? He took my hand and I almost jumped, as all the memories we had together came back. The times he took me out and we made out in a movie or went back to my house to make out in my room until my parents came home. Or the way he would tell me he loved me when he was touching me. My heart beat raced. We walked up the stairs and he stumbled a second.

"You OK?" I asked loudly over the music. He nodded and kept on walking. We walked into a dark hallway spotted with people making out. I wanted to talk to Grant and I hoped that's what would happen.

Chapter 46

We opened up the last door on the right and saw no one so we went in. It was dark and only a small light on the wall showed that it had a bed and band posters. It was a guy's room I think. Probably Jonathan's. I was about to turn around and say something when Grant's lips crashed onto mine. I was so stunned that I didn't move. He wrapped his arms around my waist and pulled me to him. His lips felt sticky and wet and the taste of beer filled my mouth. I pulled away.

"Grant," I whispered, feeling weird.

"Mm?" he asked.

"I don't think—"

"Lidia, I love you. I can't get you out of my mind. I broke up with Kendra because I want to be with you. I love the way you smile and laugh. I couldn't stand Kendra. I have to have you." He started kissing me again and this time I let him. He really felt that way for me? He was confessing his love for me. Like he did in my dreams. We sat down on the bed and he moaned in my mouth as I started kissing him back, not really closing my eyes though, still thinking. I forgot how much I liked Grant, I guess. This is what I wanted, wasn't it? Isn't it why Jack and I got together? For Jack to get Kendra back and for me to get Grant back? This is what we had planned on...right? Not having sex with Jack or falling for him! Grant pushed his tongue into my mouth and I frowned slightly at how I didn't quite like that. But I ignored it. He put his hand on my knee. I realized his hands were hard. They weren't soft. Not like Jack's. They went up my leg, not making me shiver or have goose bumps. Then his fingers were under my skirt. I shifted a little not feeling comfortable. Why was I doing this? 'Come on, Lidia! This is what you wanted! You wanted him and now you don't! What the hell is wrong with you?!' I yelled at myself. "I love you..." he murmured over my lips. "I love you

Ollie..." I frowned again. I hated that nickname! He pushed me back on the bed and I limply co-operated trying to find a reason I shouldn't want this. He pushed himself down on me and I gasped from his weight. He thought it was from the kiss and groaned. "Oh baby..." he said, turned on. I then realized something. I didn't like Grant. The feelings I was feeling, were old feelings. Not new ones. The new ones I felt were...oh my gosh! I was in love with Jack Walker! My eyes opened and I pushed Grant off me, grinning like an idiot. "What's wrong baby?" his words slurred together and I knew for a fact that he was drunk.

"Ha. Nothing. But you know what?" He leaned forward toward me trying to put his hands on me.

"What?" he asked. I pulled his hand off me and looked him straight in the eyes.

"I don't love you anymore, Grant. Actually I don't even think I like you as a person." His mouth dropped open and his eyes grew big as saucers, stunned that I would say something like that.

"What?" he asked, confused. I stood up still grinning and looked down at him.

"I was never really in love with you Grant! At least I'm pretty sure I wasn't. Maybe it was puppy love, but nothing more. But I was so interested in you that I forgot I had this deep down weird strange most interesting feeling toward Jack, this whole time!" I said throwing my hands in the air. Admitting it out loud made my heart pound and it made me want to cry with joy, or at least jump up and down like a school girl.

"You mean Walker?" Grant asked loudly. I nodded staring off at the wall. I need to tell him. Tonight. I have time. It's not too late. I need to. Then maybe we can be together. For real, for real. Oh my gosh, Jack! I've always been in love with you! I looked back down at a frowning and confused Grant.

"Grant...I got to go," I said and ran towards the door.

"Wait!" he called. I swung open the door scaring a couple in the corner.

"Oops sorry!" I said, still giddy.

"Ollie wait!" he said. I turned toward the door. He stared at me his eyes dull and his hair matted. He looked like an average guy to me.

"Oh! Sorry! I forgot to thank you." He frowned.

"The hell?" he asked. I grinned even bigger.

"Thank you for being an asshole and dumping me. If you didn't, I would still be with you. And probably unhappy. And thanks for calling me Ollie because I actually hate that name with a passion!" He was looking at me as if I was insane. The couple in the corner, I couldn't tell who they were, but they were watching and listening to us.

"You're such a bitch, Lidia!" He yelled, furious. I laughed, still grinning.

"I know!" I leaned forward and kissed his cheek then patted his arm. "But if you didn't dump me, I would be a much bigger bitch of an idiot for being with you," I confirmed. He was about to curse at me when his eyes rolled back into his head and he flopped to the ground and started snoring. I laughed then ran down the hallway at full speed. I have to go see Jack! I have to tell him how I really feel! I love him!

Chapter 47

I raced into the hospital and running down the hall toward the doors that brought me to Jack's hallway. A nurse was coming out and about to lock the doors when she turned and saw me.

"Miss visiting hours are—"

"Please!" it came out as a hoarse cry. She jumped, surprised. I grabbed the nurse by the shoulders and glanced down at her nametag. "Peggy! Listen you have GOT to let me in. The man I want to spend the rest of my life with is about 5 feet away from me and he has no idea! Please! Please! Let me in for my happiness! For the sake of my sanity!" The woman stared at me and her lips twitched.

"Miss, I was just going to say you still have an hour for visiting hours to end." I loosened my grip on her shoulder.

"Oh," I said and she smiled. I finally let her shoulder go. "I was just doing that for dramatic—"

"Go get your man!" she called, waving me to the door. I grinned.

"Thanks! Oh and sorry about the…" I pointed toward her shoulders and knew there would be a mark. She laughed.

"Just go." Without further ado, I ran into the white hallway and then stopped at Jack's room. It was shut almost the whole way but was open just a crack. I took a deep breath. You love him Lidia. And I can't believe you JUST realized that now. You're such an idiot! I just need to tell him. I pushed open the door and Jack was standing up. He looked sharply at the door his eyes were dark and his brow was furrowed like he was mad. He was perfect, though. Everything I wanted was him. I loved everything about him.

"Jack!" it came out as a gasp as I ran over to him. "I have to tell you something." I said quickly.

"That you slept with Grant at the party tonight?" he said bitterly, making me flinch.

"What?" I asked confused; losing my train of thought. "Wait, no I didn't sleep with Grant. Listen I really, really need---"

"Yeah right! I heard you were all over him!" I was puzzled, my happiness quickly leaving me.

"Jack, no, I didn't do anything with Grant. I mean we kissed but that was it. But I found something out. I—"

"So you admit that you did!" he said. "I can't believe you! You know even if we don't really like each other, you could have at least slept with someone who wasn't Grant. Way to go in making me a pathetic loser!" he yelled loudly. I stared, frozen in shock. Who did he hear this from? I didn't sleep with him! Why can't Jack let me tell him how I really feel? Why can't he know from the way I was looking at him right now? "I knew you were just like Kendra," he said so coldly that I flinched again. He towered over me and I felt like I was filled with coldness. He doesn't love or like me now. Tears filled my eyes.

"Jack...I didn't—"

"You know!" he said cutting me off and stepping back away from me. His eyes were black and I felt like no warmth could ever come to me again. "Save it. I don't care about anything you say. We can basically say this stupid, idiotic, pointless fake relationship is over!" he said, slicing his hand through the air to modify it was over. It was silent. I stared at the ground tears falling helplessly. I can't let him do this to me. I thought. I can't let him cut me like this. I looked up and I saw his body lose its stiffness. Find your strength Lidia. Find it now!

"The fake relationship was your idea!" I yelled. He glared. "You're the one who approached me and asked me! Don't you forget that!" I pointed a finger. Then I stepped back feeling like my legs were Jell-O. They won't support me for long. I quieted my voice as I stared straight into his eyes. He saw it coming. He knew. "Pointless? I guess you think my virginity was pointless?" It was silent and he didn't say anything. I clenched my teeth. Be strong. Do not show him you're about to barf everything you ate today onto the floor, or that your heart hurts like someone stabbed a pen through it. Act like you stubbed your toe and it's the aftereffects. I bit the inside of my mouth hard with my hands already in fist. I stepped back again and looked at him. Without another word from either of us, I left. I didn't even bother to stop as I started running. I ran outside and into the cold air hoping it would help the hard sobs that hurt my chest so bad I wanted to scream.

Jack

Oh damn. I can't believe I just did that! Oh man...I will never forget that look Lidia gave me. That sad broken-hearted look. I shook my head.

"Get it out of your head!" I yelled out loud. She broke your heart, you stupid person! She cheated on you with Grant! I will thank Greg the next time I see him. He said he was standing there next to Grant when Lidia walked up and told him to come upstairs with her. She was practically throwing herself at him! Why shouldn't I be mad? Greg was Grant's good friend and I hated the jock, but why would he lie to me? He actually was nice enough to come and warn me. I should be happy. But I'm more upset than I thought I would be. I waited in bed thinking maybe she would come over after the party and tell me she had a good time and all, then I would confront her and yell at her and she would admit that she cheated on me and then she would beg for forgiveness. But she didn't. She just listened trying to tell me something. I didn't care what she had to tell me! I was downright pissed! She was making me look a fool! Maybe she's been seeing Grant all this time. Greg also told me that Grant and Kendra broke up. Why didn't Lidia tell me that?! I crushed my hands to my head feeling the head spasms. I can't believe what I'd just said to Lidia. I couldn't help it. It all sort of rushed out. I felt like I was yelling at Kendra. Or maybe that's what I wanted to do. But, still. Lidia hurt me more then she knew and she didn't even care! I had the right to be angry. A bigger right then she did…because I actually fell for her.

Lidia

I wanted my mom. I wanted to feel her warm embrace. Like I did when I was five and a thunderstorm was coming in and lightening made the sky light and scary. Then the thunder rumbled and I would push my face into my mother's neck trying to get away from it. She would shush me telling me that it was alright. Then dad would tell me that it was okay and rub my back. I wanted both my parents more than anything right now. I wanted to be five again and be running from a thunderstorm, than having my heart torn in two. I jumped out of the car and ran to the door. It was locked. I quickly unlocked it, sobs breaking my chest. I threw open the door and stumbled in. The lights were turned off and everything was quiet. No one was home. With a sick retching sob I screamed. I'm sure the whole neighborhood could hear it. I didn't care.

"Why is no one home when I need them the most?" I screamed as I raced toward the fire place ripping off the stockings with our names on them.

"Why is it that my parents don't give a rat's ass about me?" I screamed as I kicked a picture frame of us in Paris smiling on one of the stands. I ran toward the staircase where the pretty ribbon was wrapped around the railing. I pulled it off, ripping it, making a tearing sound.

"Why can't my parents care more about me then themselves?" I was in rage and nothing could stop me! I ran toward the Christmas tree we had gotten and glared up at it.

"Why can't Jack listen to me?" With another blow of rage, I knocked down the Christmas tree and all the ornaments fell and shattered. With that, my legs finally gave out and I crumpled to the ground. I held myself tightly together as I let out the last cries.

Afterwards my hands bled from the glass as I picked it up. I threw it away with a blank expression. I had to get out of there. I went up the stairs and into my room grabbed a big, black duffle bag and threw my clothes in it. As I passed the mirror, I stopped and stared at myself. My makeup had come off and made my cheeks black with eyeliner. My tight shirt and skirt felt almost claustrophobic. I didn't look like myself. I hadn't for a while now. Since I wanted to make Grant jealous, I had changed my whole personality. 'I hate this person,' I thought, looking in the mirror. I couldn't believe I let Grant walk all over me like that! He was controlling me and I didn't even know. But the time when I felt most like myself was when I was with Jack. I felt braver and stronger when I was with him. 'Don't think about him,' I told myself. With another set of rage, I tore my black skirt taking it off along with my shirt. I yanked it off hearing it tear here and there. I slipped on a pair of jeans and a warm sweat shirt. I got everything I needed from the bathroom and then wrote a note. Before I left, I went to my jewelry box and opened it. A picture of my grandma and I sat smiling at me. I didn't smile back; I grabbed the key and shut it. I put my duffle bag over my shoulder and headed out to my jeep. I needed to get away from it. I needed to get fresh air.

Lidia's note---

Mom and Dad,

I'm going away for a while. I just can't be home. If you need me you can call the cabin phone number because I don't get reception there. Please, don't come up. I just want to be alone for the holidays like every year. I'll call you when I get there. Love you both.

Lidia

Chapter 48

I stayed at the cabin for two weeks. I smiled as I ran my fingers over the soft old sofa. It felt smooth and just how I remembered it when I was 8. I looked at the coffee stain on the floor and put my head on the arm of the sofa to stare at it. I remember that. My grandma had given me a taste of her coffee and me being only 4, I wanted a little more. The cup tipped back too far and it got all over my face and then I dropped the cup and screamed because it was a little hot. It stained the floor. I closed my eyes and I swore I could almost hear my grandma humming in the kitchen and the sound of the microwave being turned on as she heated a cup of coffee or tea. But I could hear nothing. I reopened my eyes and looked at the fireplace in front of me. There were no Christmas decorations, no Christmas tree or any presents. Just a fireplace. Christmas was over, but sometimes you could still feel like it was still there. The smell, the sound...but no. There was nothing. The only thing I did for Christmas was make myself a small turkey and mashed potatoes. Plus, I went into the closest town and bought myself a couple of books. The TV there only had 5 channels. My mom had called at midnight the day I got there. She was worried, of course. But I wouldn't tell her what was wrong. After that, she called once a day and then later, once every couple of days. I hadn't heard anything from Jack at all and I was pretty sure I wouldn't either. School would be starting back soon. Tomorrow, actually. Today was New Year's. I could hear fireworks going off miles away. I stood up and walked to the window, pulling my sleeves down around my fingers and watched fireworks shoot up from the towns below me.

Jack

I watched the fireworks as one of the moronic party-goers threw a firework and it bounced back to hit him in the leg. He screamed. I sighed and took another long drink of my beer. I was released from the hospital a week ago and was mostly better. The bastard Scott was in jail for a couple years and my mom was happy. But I wasn't. I didn't know why, though. I should be happy that Lidia and I aren't together. She cheated on me! No bitch cheats on Jack Walker! I clenched my hands tightly. But Lidia isn't a bitch. I thought I was in—

"Yo Jack! Want to take a crack at this?" one of the guys asked, holding up a fancy firework. I shook my head. He laughed and lit it himself. I didn't know how she was doing and she hadn't tried to call me. I didn't either. I wanted to see her. I wanted to tell her that I forgave her, but I couldn't. I thought we had something going till she decided to have sex with Grant. It hurt. More than anything in my life. Not even Scott putting me in the hospital hurt as much as that. I sighed and took another drink.

"Hey, honey," said a sly voice. I looked over and saw some stupid blonde cheerleader in a tight skirt walking over to me. I raised an eyebrow. "How are you? Heard you and that girl broke up." I shrugged.

"Fine. And yeah," I said, not caring. She came up and pressed her body on the side of mine, making sure I felt her boobs on my arm.

"Want to go have a little party of our own?" she asked, batting her eye lashes at me. She wasn't pretty. She wore gobs of makeup and her lips were bright red and some was on her chin. She also smelled like beer. I thought of Lidia kissing Grant and smirked at the ground. I then looked up at the cheerleader and grinned.

"I like parties." She smiled seductively and took my hand. If Lidia can play this game, so can I. The girl pulled me forward quickly as we rounded the porch and then walked across the yard to the tool shed. I grimaced slightly. I hated these kinds of places but, oh well. She pulled me into the shed and it smelled like ground. She slammed the door shut and I could barely see her as she grabbed my face. It was dark but some of the light from the house seeped through. She kissed me roughly and moaned into my mouth. Her hands were cold on my neck and I felt weird for a moment. Lidia didn't kiss like this. She was rough. Lidia's lips were gentle...Don't think about her! You're making out with another girl! I put my hands around the girl's waist and pulled her to me. She was little and there was barely anything to hold on to. I didn't like it. Lidia was taller and I didn't have to bend my head down this low or have my whole hand fit around this girl's stomach. She bit my lip, moaning again and then bit my chin. It hurt. She tasted of beer and strawberries. Rotten strawberries. She put her hands on my chest and slipped her hands under my shirt, feeling my abs.

"Oh, you are so hot!" she sang, feeling every curve. "I just want to eat you!" she practically ripped off my shirt and I grunted. Oh man, this is just weird. I don't even know this girl's name and I'm about to have sex with her! For only my second time. I don't even know if I did it right the first time! I guess I did, I mean Lidia didn't complain about it. Though, I don't think she would have. She's too nice of a person. Ugh! Stop it! With anger I felt for her I put my hand under the girl's skirt and grabbed her thigh. "Oh yes!" she gasped between her tongue in my mouth. She lifted her leg and hooked it around mine. "Ugh, do that again," she coed. I grabbed her thigh. "Closer." She whispered. I put my hand further up her skirt and I felt the heat from her. I squeezed. "Jack, baby!" she screamed arching her back, her body very close to mine, rubbing me inside my jeans. It didn't really turn me on, though. She pulled away from me and yanked off her shirt clumsily. A flash from the night with Lidia came across my eyes as the girl put her lips back on mine. Lidia's slight smile as she straddled me and pulled up her shirt. Then as she bent down to kiss me sweetly with her eyes tightly shut.

"Lidia..." I whispered. The girl pulled back.

"What?" she asked. I swallowed.

"Nothing."

She stared for a minute and then shrugged.

"I want your pants off," she breathed, putting her hands on the top of my jeans. I bit my lip.

"Yeah," I said. She yanked off my belt then unzipped my pants and pulled them down. She licked my leg as she came back up.

I jumped slightly surprised. She grinned at me and then unclipped her bra. Her breasts fell out. They were really tiny. I remembered Lidia's. How nice they were. Just perfect. I shook my head. Don't, Jack. She latched onto me, throwing her whole body around me. She licked and kissed my neck as I held onto her, trying not to fall over. Again, a picture of Lidia smiling and laughing filled my vision. Her pretty eyes, the way they glowed when she saw something she liked. The way she would frown if something bothered her. The way she would look off into the distance in her own world, not caring what was happening in this one. I opened my eyes and dropped the girl who clung to me. She gasped.

"What?" she asked, annoyed. I clenched my teeth. You're such an idiot! She cheated on you but you still can't have sex with anyone else! You're worthless.

"I can't," I said. I grabbed my clothes and put them on.

"What did you just say to me?" the cheerleader asked. I zipped up my pants. I got chills from the snow outside. I couldn't believe I didn't feel that till now. Must have been thinking too much.

"I said, I don't want to have sex with you. I'm going." I pushed past her while putting on my jacket. I had found it folded up on the brown chair Lidia used to sit on in the hospital. I asked the nurse about it and she said a girl gave it to her at the desk.

"You're such a loser!" the girl called out at me. I just ignored her and walked back to my car.

I woke up with a giant headache and groaned. No, no, no! Damn, I had to get a hangover EVERY time I got drunk! Bloody sucks. I slapped my alarm and it went on snooze for the 13th time.

"Jack...," Mom said outside my door.

"No," I said sleepily. I heard my door creak open.

"Jack, get up. It's getting late." I ignored her and shoved my face into the pillow. "Jack, get up!" she yelled. I winced, but ignored her. Then I heard her walk away. Ha-ha! I started to fall back into sleep as I heard my name being called again. Then before I knew it a wooden spoon was pounding on a metal pan, ringing in through my ears. I jumped up quickly screaming, and then fell face first onto the floor. "That's what you get for drinking," Mom said smugly.

I went to school after popping 4 Aspirins into my mouth and putting on a pair of sunglasses. I walked in slowly, trying not to slap my feet on the ground because it hurt my ears.

"Hey Jack!" one of my friends called, putting out his hand for me to slap. I ignored him and walked to my locker. I didn't want to talk to anyone today. People murmured around me but I just pretended I didn't care. Someone tapped my back.

"Jack." A quiet voice said. I ignored them. "Jack!" she yelled. She pulled my shoulder and Kendra looked me straight in the eyes. She looked like shit. She had dark purple lines under her eyes and her hair was a mess. "Would you stop being arrogant?! I don't want to yell, it hurts too much," she said, closing her eyes for a second. She was hung-over too.

"What do you want, then?" I asked bitterly. She flinched slightly. Either from me saying it too loudly or because it was mean. Both would be good to me. I could care less to even talk to this girl again.

"I want to talk to you about Lidia."

"Kendra, leave me the hell alone," I warned as I stepped around her.

"Jack, wait!" she yelled.

"Oh! Damn! That hurt!" she said, stopping to hold her head. The bell rang and we both grabbed our ears. Kids left the hallways. I started for my class, ignoring her. "Jack, stop!" She ran up and grabbed me roughly.

"Ow!" I yelled.

"Come with me," she ordered strongly. She pulled me across the school and pushed me into a closet.

"What the hell do you want?!" I yelled. She pushed me back. I hit the wall and stared wide eyed at her. She looked pissed.

"You listen to me! I'm trying to tell you something and you are being a jerk!" I was surprised.

"Fine," I said like a child. She huffed.

"Lidia didn't have sex with Grant." I snorted and rolled my eyes standing back up again.

"Yeah rig—"

"You shut the freak up and listen!" she pushed me back again. I stumbled and fell to my butt. She glared down at me. "Don't even say another word!" she warned. "Lidia did the exact opposite! She told Grant that she did NOT and I repeat NOT like him and she thanked him for dumping her." I frowned up at her.

"Why would she thank him?" Kendra's face softened.

"Because she said she fell in love with you."

My heart stopped. Never in my life did I think I would hear that from Lidia. I stared dumbfounded. Oh god, I said really mean stuff to her. I...that's why she came so late! She wanted to tell me something! She was going to tell me that.

"Oh, man," I said putting my hands to my face.

"Yeah exactly!" Kendra said.

"What did I do?" I asked myself out loud. Kendra sighed. "How do you know this?" I asked looking up at her.

"I was making out in the hallway when she came running out of the room with Grant, telling him off and saying she had to go find you." I clenched my teeth. I've screwed everything up.

"Why are you doing this?" I asked. She frowned slightly.

"Because, even if we haven't been getting along, I still love her. She was like my sister. I couldn't let her get hurt again. Even if the first time was my fault." She looked down, frowning. Her eyes got misty. "I screwed our friendship up because of a guy." She laughed coldly. "I'm an idiot."

I looked up at her. Maybe she wasn't as bad as I thought. She was just as screwed as I was. I didn't feel anything for her romantically, but I could maybe think we could be friends sometime.

"I need to go talk to her." I said, standing up, feeling determined.

"Yeah...wait!" she said as I reached for the door.

"What?"

"I forgot! Lidia isn't at school or home." I frowned.

"Then where the hell is she?" I asked annoyed.

She bit her lip.

"I called her and her parents said that she left two weeks ago. Said she went to see her grandma or something? Or someplace around the mountains? I can't remember." Why would she go to her grandma's?

"And she's not here today?" I asked. She shook her head with a sad expression. "Damn!" I said and opened the door. Where would she be around the mountains..? "Oh! I know where she is!" I said thinking back to our little... "There is this great place I know of. It's up around the mountains somewhere. My grandma used to take me up there and we would stay there for a week or two on holidays when my parents went away. It was always so beautiful in the winter..."

225

Chapter 49

"I've got to get that address," I said, clenching my hands. Kendra looked at me and smiled sadly.

"I always knew you were a good person." I gave her a small smile. "I'm sorry for what happened between us," Kendra said quietly. I nodded.

"Yeah, me too." She kissed my cheek softly in a friendly way.

"Go after her and tell her how you feel." I grinned.

"Don't worry, I will!"

She laughed as I turned around and ran.

"Can you please tell me the address? I need it! If I don't talk to her, I will rip out my heart and feed it to the animals!" I said dramatically. Mrs. Taylor stared at me with wide eyes.

"I said I would give it to you, Jack, sweetie." I guess this is why Lidia tells me I'm dramatic.

"Oh...OK. Well, can I have it right now?"

She nodded.

Lidia

I opened the front door and stepped out and the cold winter air hit me softly. I pulled my jacket around me more securely. It was a nice day. Warmer than usual. I didn't want to go back home today. It was the first day of school and mom had finally called to remind me. I told her to tell them I was sick for the next 4 days. I didn't want to have to go back to school and see Jack. I couldn't stand just seeing him and not being able to touch him. I didn't want to break down in tears when he looked at me, if he did at all. I hate being weak! And he was my weakness. And I let him take it and he abused it. My feet crunched as I walked across the hard snow, past my Jeep and up along the ridge of the mountain. I exhaled as I looked out across the mountains to the city. It was beautiful! The big hills had snow covering their peaks and the sky was blue with a couple of clouds dotting it. The aroma in the air reminded me of when I was a kid and Grandma would bring me out here and we would sit and watch the sunset. I closed my eyes as the sun warmed my face and the wind blew my hair back. I could hear me as a kid talking to my grandma......

"Grandmamma, why does the sun always set?" She would sigh and kiss my cheek as I rested in her lap.

"Because that's the way God intended it to be. It is the way of life. It sometimes can be sad, but remember: every sunset comes to an end with someone you love. And honey, everything comes to an end at some time." I frowned, turning to look up at her.

"Does everybody's life come to an end, Grandmamma?" she smiled sadly at me.

"Yes, baby. But that's not the end." I smiled.

"Good! Because I want to live with my family forever!" Grandma laughed and nestled me closer.

A tear fell down my cheek as I just shut my eyes and fought to keep myself from missing the memory of my Grand mamma's arms wrapped around me. I sighed and opened my eyes. They were burning from me fighting the tears. "Every sunset comes to an end with someone you love...or without one." I whispered my Grand mama's words. The last part, I added on. Because it was the truth. Truth hurts people the most. I wiped my cheek and smiled at the white cross with a purple bow on saying my grandma's name. I walked back through the trees just as I heard a car come roaring up the road. I stopped dead in my tracks at the edge of the driveway. The familiar orange Camaro bouncing feverishly around looking like everything would fall apart if it didn't stop, came up my driveway. I stared, my heart rate increasing. How?

Chapter 50

Jack jumped out from the car. His eyes were bright blue. I'd forgotten how bright they could be. They jolted my insides. He was wearing his leather jacket, faded jeans and cowboy boots. I needed to own him. He slammed his car door shut, ran up the driveway and stopped several feet away from me. He stared at me, his jaw clenched. He was looking all over me with that weird look in his eyes. Why was he here? He hurt me! Was he here to make it worse?

"Lidia," he finally said, looking into my eyes. The name made my stomach flutter. No, don't let him do this to you. You're not going to be weak anymore. Before he could say anymore I turned and started to go around him, my head low with my hair covering my face. "Lidia, stop!" he yelled, but did not touch me. I stopped and turned back to him. I didn't want to talk. Why did he have to come here? I was finally getting over him and he had to come and ruin it! I wanted to be left alone. "We have to talk! It's important. I know you didn't have sex with Grant." I clenched my teeth till I bit the inside of my mouth. I was not going to talk. I will not talk to him. Why couldn't he have just believed me when I told him? I started walking again. "Lidia!" he yelled. Before I could reach the steps, he caught up and spun me around. "Don't you do this to me, Lidia Taylor," he growled. He shook my shoulders till I glared up at him, still not speaking. "You are always running away! Don't you dare shut down on me." I was mad. I pulled my hand up and hit him across the face. His head flew to the side and he closed his eyes and let go of my shoulder to hold his jaw. I was steaming with anger by the time he flexed his jaw and looked at me, a grin at his lips. I frowned. Why was he grinning? "Nice hit...for a girl." This tipped me over the edge. Screw not talking.

"I'll show you how a real girl hits!" I pulled my hand back up but he grabbed it and pulled me close to him, smashing his lips to mine. It felt so good, but I couldn't let this go. With all my might I pushed him back and he frowned. "Don't," I threatened. He frowned.

"I said I believe that you didn't cheat on me. Lidia, please, I was an idiot!" he pleaded. I felt myself softening. I can't. No, not now. "Please forgive me?"

I stared at him.

"I did. Many times before, Jack. But this is bigger than getting into a little fight about bruises." My hands fell at my sides feeling like crap. We will never be able to have a real relationship. "I thought we trusted each other. I thought you would never listen to any stupid thing someone said about me cheating on you. I would never." I whispered the last words. "You didn't trust me. I learned after finding out about Kendra and Grant having something when they were dating us, that I would never hurt anyone as much as they did." But fighting with you hurts more. I looked down clearing my throat of the hollowness.

"I'm sorry," Jack said quietly sounding like he would break down any moment. "I screw up everything good that comes to me," he whispered. It was over. It was done. I felt a weight lift off me but emptiness came in its place. I wanted to go back inside and forget this happened. "But one thing," I looked up at Jack as he raised his head to look at me. "That I didn't screw up was that I met you and we got into the fake relationship." I was surprised. "Lidia, that was the happiest I've been in my life. It was when I was with you...on that snowy night..." My heart jumped, getting a fast pace. What was he saying? His blue eyes softened and the cold air made his lips a little purple and his hair flew back out of his eyes. He was beautiful. "Lidia...I've been in love with you for a long time now." The words sent a small gasp out of my mouth. He loves me! He feels the same way I feel about him! I stared, shocked out of my mind! He stepped closer. "Ever since I met you, I knew I was going to love you no matter how many times we fought, or how many times we said we hated each other." He stepped closer and the distance was done. He was so close I could feel his warm breath on me. Oh, God, how I loved him, too. 'Tell him!' I told myself. I licked my lips and before I could say anything his were on mine. This time I didn't push him away. He put his hands on my back bringing me closer as I weaved my hands in his hair. Oh that soft hair! I missed him so much! I can't believe I'm giving in this quickly!

"God, I hate you," I muttered as his lips kissed me again. He laughed knowing he'd won. I sucked on his lip. I could taste him. The peppermint and just a slight bitterness of cigarettes. He pulled back and we were both panting. He leaned his forehead on mine.

"How about some of that fun we talked about having?" I laughed.

"Let's." He picked me up, looking into my eyes and that's when I realized what that gleam was. His love for me. He pushed open the cabin door and shut it. I kissed his neck and collarbone. I had forgotten how good he tasted! He walked back to the hall guessing at where the bedroom was. When he found it he put me down to my feet. He cupped my cheek. I wrestled with the button on his jacket, feeling my body heat up.

"I missed you so much," he whispered. I smiled.

"I missed you. Now please can we get these clothes off?"

He grinned and laughed as he unbuttoned his jacket and then threw off his shirt. I tore off my jacket and shirt. He smiled softly as he pulled me to him. I kissed his chest. He laughed. I pulled him over to the bed and he climbed on top of me.

"Now how does the fun go?" I asked, gleaming.

He fell off to the side of me, sweat beading his forehead. I looked over and smiled. I loved him. I knew deep in my heart that we were going to be together for the rest of our lives. He looked over at me and his blue eyes were soft and sweet. I smiled and put my fingers on his lips. I traced them and then I looked back into his eyes.

"Tired already?" I asked.

He smiled.

"Not even close."

We sat on the ledge looking out over the beautiful mountains. I was in between his legs with his arms around my body, hugging me closely. I did not want this day to end. He kissed my head. The wind blew the breeze at us. I touched his hand that was around me and leaned back. He put his chin on my shoulder and I felt stubble from his cheek.

"I love you," he said.

"I love you, too, Jack." I finally confessed to him

"I know, Princess." We both laughed at the nickname.

"I loved being in a fake relationship with you," Jack sighed laughing a little, "but now the real thing is beyond anything I ever expected!"

I laughed too, knowing that's exactly what I was thinking......

The End

Thank You

Dear Reader,

Thank you for choosing to read my books out of the thousands that merit reading. I recognize that reading takes time and quietness, so I am grateful that you have designed your lives to allow for this enriching endeavor, whatever the book's title and subject.

Now more than ever before, Amazon reviews and Social Media play vital role in helping individuals make their reading choices. If any of my books have moved you, inspired you, or educated you, please share your reactions with others by posting an Amazon review as well as via email, Facebook, Twitter, Goodreads, -- or even old-fashioned face-to-face conversation!

I invite you to connect with me on Facebook:

https://www.facebook.com/Author-Paige-Powers-848643855286645/

With profound gratitude, and with hope for your continued reading pleasure,

Paige Powers

Author & Publisher

Printed in Great Britain
by Amazon

36470746R00139